GHOULFRIENDS
'til the end

ALSO BY
GITTY DANESHVARI

Ghoulfriends Forever

Ghoulfriends Just Want to Have Fun

Who's That Ghoulfriend?

School of Fear

School of Fear: Class Is NOT Dismissed!

School of Fear: The Final Exam

MONSTER HIGH

GHOULFRIENDS
'til the end

WRITTEN BY
GITTY DANESHVARI

ILLUSTRATED BY
DARKO DORDEVIC

LITTLE, BROWN AND COMPANY
NEW YORK • BOSTON

Little, Brown and Company

Hachette Book Group
237 Park Avenue, New York, NY 10017
Visit our website at lb-kids.com

Little, Brown and Company is a division of Hachette Book Group, Inc.
The Little, Brown name and logo are trademarks of Hachette Book Group, Inc.

The publisher is not responsible for websites (or their content) that are not owned by the publisher.

First Edition: April 2014

Library of Congress Control Number: 2013033907

ISBN 978-0-316-22251-8

10 9 8 7 6 5 4 3 2 1

RRD-C

Printed in the United States of America

For Edwin "Win" Shames.
I can't wait to introduce you
to your first deli cat.

CHAPTER one

 sudden gust of wind pushed through the thick green conifurs lining the edge of campus, curved around the imposing stone and glass facade of Monster High, and finally swept across the backfield. A welcome respite from the intensity of the sun, the breeze delighted the throngs of athletically clad students as Crack and Shield Day got under way.

"Welcome to the Ghoul's Cry Jump, a competition to see who could simultaneously jump the highest while shrieking the loudest," Monster High's Deputy of Disaster and acting headmistress, Miss Sue Nami, yelled into a bullhorn.

On the field, eager to participate, were Venus McFlytrap, Robecca Steam, Rochelle Goyle, Scarah Screams, Cleo de Nile, and Toralei Stripe, all of whom were wearing matching Monster High helmets.

"First up is Rochelle Goyle," the waterlogged and box-shaped woman barked as she looked over at the petite granite gargoyle with small white wings.

Upon hearing her name, Rochelle quickly pulled back her long pink hair, brushed aside her turquoise-streaked bangs, and waved hello to the crowd. Acting more like a visiting dignitary than an athlete, she performed a full three-sixty before heading to the starting line. Seconds after she double-checked her helmet and assumed the correct position, the starting gun fired. Rochelle sprinted with all her might, thrust herself into the air, and screamed at the top of her lungs.

"Holy mackerel, who knew Rochelle had those kind of pipes?" Robecca Steam muttered as wisps of steam wafted out of her copper-plated ears.

Crafted from a steam engine by her mad-scientist father, the blue-haired ghoul released steam whenever overcome by a strong emotion, whether it be excitement, fear, or anger.

"I know, right? If only she could get her granite body a little higher in the air," Venus, the jade-skinned daughter of the plant monster, replied.

The long-pink-and-green-haired ghoul then began to stretch her legs while warming up her vocal cords.

"*Do-re-mi-fa-sol-la-ti*," Venus sang quietly as Miss Sue Nami lifted the bullhorn to her mouth.

"Toralei Stripe and Cleo de Nile, you are disqualified for refusing to unlink your arms. Get off the field!" Miss Sue Nami screeched at the two pouting divas.

"*C'est incroyable*! I can't believe those two are still linking arms," Rochelle said as she walked up to Robecca and Venus.

"They think they're less likely to be kidnapped by the normies if they're together," Venus responded, shaking her head incredulously. "It's crazy how everyone has bought this normie story hook, line, and sinker."

Following banshee Scarah Screams's winning turn in the Cry Jump, Robecca, Rochelle, and Venus decided it was time to track down another ghoul, one who just might prove useful in bringing Monster High's era of doom and gloom to an end. And so the trio zigzagged through hordes of monsters, their eyes darting from side to side in search of Wydowna Spider.

"Ghouls? Do you think it will ever be normal at Monster High? Maybe even a little boring?" Robecca asked Venus and Rochelle while moving past a couple of sea creatures mid-stretch.

"*Chérie*, I wish I could say yes, but just think of all that's happened since we arrived at Monster High. First Madame Flapper cast that terrible spell—the Whisper—that robbed all the students and teachers of their ability to think for themselves! *Quelle horreur!*"

"I have to say, breaking that spell was not easy," Venus recalled. "And to think, Miss Flapper just walked away free and clear after claiming that she too had been under a spell! What a load of fertilizer!"

"It sure was stranger than a bee's-sneeze-in-a-strong-breeze how quickly everyone went back to business as usual. Why, even the appearance of white kittens and dolls of doom with messages warning of *them* failed to raise the flag," Robecca remembered aloud.

"What flag would that be?" Rochelle inquired curiously.

"Jeepers, Rochelle! There's no flag; it's just a saying," Robecca explained with a smirk.

"All these sayings. They really are terribly irksome."

"It wasn't until the graffiti messages about *them* started popping up that anyone even really paid attention. And then, of course, when Headmistress Bloodgood was kidnapped, things really got out of control," Venus added.

"Ah! And that note! That ridiculous note that claimed the normies took Headmistress Bloodgood and that they wouldn't return her until a wall had been built enclosing Salem." Rochelle moaned at the absurdity of the story.

"But everyone thinks it's true. We're pretty much the only ones who don't believe it. The others don't even suspect that Miss Flapper is working with this secret organization. As a matter of fact, they don't even know ASOME exists! Not that we know who is behind ASOME or what they're after . . ." Venus trailed off.

"But hopefully Wydowna will tell us," Rochelle chimed in.

Wydowna Spider, the daughter of Arachne, had been found living in Monster High's attic a few weeks earlier. And though at first Scariff Fred Onarrival thought she might be working for the normies as a spy, he soon accepted her story that she was just a stowaway eager to learn. But, alas, that was not the truth.

Long and lithe with onyx skin, flame-colored hair, and six arms, Wydowna kept her eyes—all six of them—trained on the ground after spotting Robecca, Rochelle, and Venus.

"We know what you're doing," Venus pressed Wydowna. "We know that you are working with Miss Flapper and ASOME. We just don't understand why you're doing it."

"I don't know what you mean," Wydowna uttered nervously.

"Stop pretending, Wydowna," Robecca said quietly.

"I'm not pretending. . . . I don't know," Wydowna whispered as she looked to her pet fly, Shoo.

"You seem so nice, so genuine. How did you get caught up in something like this? A society that holds some creatures above others? That's not right and you know it," Venus pleaded with the ghoul.

"You don't understand," Wydowna babbled as she began to cry. "I thought I was being sent here to help monsters. For the good of the whole monster world. But then I started reading things . . . things I didn't like or even understand . . ."

"Just tell us who is behind ASOME!" Venus urged the frightened spider ghoul to reveal her secrets.

"I can't tell you. It's too dangerous."

"You must tell us! The future of every ghoul and guy at Monster High depends on it!" Rochelle begged. "*S'il ghoul plaît*, Wydowna."

"You don't understand how powerful they are," Wydowna insisted.

"Just tell us who they are! We can handle them!" Venus cried out. Her nerves were completely frayed.

"You don't get it. You won't be able to stop them!" Wydowna argued.

"We stopped Miss Flapper's Whisper, and we're going to stop this too," Venus stated assuredly.

"Don't you see? It's all part of the same plan."

"What plan?" Robecca asked nervously, steam pouring out of her ears.

"You don't have a clue how far up this goes, how

long this plan has been in the making," Wydowna said as a loud siren cut through the air.

Similar to that of an air raid, the drawn-out howl seamlessly dissolved the crowd into masses of confusion and fear.

CHAPTER two

his is not a drill. I repeat, this is not a drill. All students and staff members are to report to the gymnasium for lockdown!"

It was the voice of Skultastic Superintendent Petra Fied, a tall and lanky mummy who was as expressionless and blank-faced as ever.

"Students are to report to the gymnasium now! I repeat, now!" Superintendent Petra continued as pandemonium ripped through the masses of students. Screams, flailing limbs, and even clawing abounded as the monsters fled the field. Never mind that they didn't know what the siren was for; as far as they were concerned they were running for their lives.

"Students, there is no time for trifling, walking, or chatting! We are in the throes of a code dead! Not a code yellow! Not a code orange! A code dead!!"

The use of the term *code dead* immediately amplified the hysteria, prompting the already frenzied crowd to start running around like bats in the sunlight. But upon closer inspection, one could see that not everyone was responding to the superintendent's instructions. There, in the midst of all the commotion, stood four serenely still ghouls. Much like the eye of a storm, they were static as everything moved around them.

Robecca, Venus, and Rochelle were the picture of tranquility as they stared down Wydowna, silently pleading for her to fess up. Clearly agitated, Venus felt her pollens of persuasion starting to rumble. Eager to control them, at least until absolutely necessary, she quickly closed her eyes and took a deep breath. However, just as the ghoul closed her eyes she felt a soft slap to the back of her head. It was the fabric-covered arm of Hoodude Voodoo, a life-size voodoo doll.

"Frankie!!! Frankie!!!" Hoodude hollered as he charged across the field.

"Hoodude! Take my hand!" Frankie Stein, Hoodude's creator and consummate crush, screamed while barreling across the lawn.

"Wydowna . . ." Venus started, but quickly found herself drowned out by a booming voice.

"Move it, zombie!" an impatient werewolf roared as he pushed the slow-moving creature out of the way. "Code dead means there's no time for slow-pokes!"

"I'm about ready to pollinate this whole crowd one monster at a time," Venus said, brimming with frustration.

"Steamers, that sure would be a whole lot of sneezing," Robecca muttered to herself as two pumpkin heads passed by, their large orange jack-o'-lantern heads bobbing violently atop their minuscule bodies.

"*Listen to the master and run a bit faster!*" the descendants of the Headless Horseman sang.

"Look around you, Wydowna," Venus said loudly as she did her absolute best to ignore the near-deafening cries of her classmates. "You helped start this. . . ."

"*J'ai une idée*. It might be *plus facile*, that is, easier, if you just sneeze on Wydowna. Your pollens of persuasion will surely prompt her to give us the information we need," Rochelle whispered to Venus in her delightful Scarisian accent.

"Spider monsters are immune to pollens of persuasion, and as you've probably realized by now, we also have extra-sensitive hearing," Wydowna responded while continuing to stare at the ground.

Venus's vines tightened with irritation as she

steadied herself against the barrage of creatures bumping into her while fleeing the field.

"Wydowna, *chérie*," Rochelle said with genuine kindness. "Tell us who is behind this. We know you aren't a bad ghoul."

It was an odd thing for the ever-rational Rochelle to say. Especially as she was one for facts above feelings; but in this case Rochelle could not deny what she saw in Wydowna—a good heart. Sure, she had been caught living in the attic, a supposed stowaway looking to advance her education. And sure, Rochelle knew the truth about her, that she had been working with Miss Flapper and some secret organization called ASOME to try to destroy Monster High. And yet still, Rochelle sensed that Wydowna was not the enemy.

"We need the truth about ASOME in order to

stop them. Who are they? Who are you and Miss Flapper working for?" Venus pleaded as she reached out and touched Wydowna's shimmery black arm.

"I thought I was helping monsters," Wydowna uttered emphatically, her six eyes still locked on the ground. "I believed them when they said that I was protecting future generations, securing a brighter future for monsters everywhere."

"But now you know that you were not in fact helping monsters, so it's time to do the right thing," Rochelle implored Wydowna while tapping her sharp stone claws against her leg.

"I bet the normies are coming! That's why they sounded the alarm! Run, monsters, run!" Henry Hunchback hollered as he sprinted hump-first toward Monster High's main building.

Robecca, Rochelle, and Venus knew that it

was not the normies who had taken Headmistress Bloodgood. They also knew that the normies were not the ones behind the threats of walling off Salem. The only problem was, they couldn't prove any of it. They needed Wydowna's help to identify the members of the secret organization pulling the strings.

"Rochelle!" Deuce Gorgon called out from a swarm of sea creatures. "Come on! I just heard the normies are coming! Word is they're going to try and kidnap as many of us as possible!"

"She'll catch up with you in a second," Venus replied casually, much to the boy's surprise.

"But, but . . ." Deuce stuttered from behind his ever-present sunglasses.

"See you soon, D," Venus said with a friendly

20

wave as the boy with a snake Mohawk disappeared into the crowd.

"Heavens to batsy, Wydowna! This is your moment! You can stop it before it's too late!" Robecca hollered, and then flipped the switch to her rocket boots and soared into the air to avoid a manic werewolf headed straight for her.

"I'm afraid it's already too late," Wydowna said while shaking her head.

"It's never too late to do the right thing! *Absolument jamais!*" Rochelle responded sincerely as Robecca returned to the ground.

"ASOME is powerful, connected in ways you could never imagine, with moles everywhere. They'll do anything to protect the creature hierarchy that they believe in. Anything."

"Let us at least try to save our headmistress, our

school, our town from whatever it is that they're planning," Rochelle begged.

Wydowna lifted her head, stared directly at each of the ghouls, and parted her lips to answer. Anticipation immediately seized Rochelle, Robecca, and Venus as they saw that she was finally ready to tell them the truth.

"ASOME is—" Wydowna said, before being slammed by a river of frantic vampires storming across the lawn.

At first Wydowna's onyx skin made it easy to track her in the sea of pale monsters, but as the group moved faster, the trio lost sight of even the smallest swath of black.

"I'll follow her in the air!" Robecca offered as she bent down to flip on her boots again.

"Save your fuel. We know where she's headed,

where all of them are headed," Venus said as she motioned to start walking.

"Let's just hope that Wydowna doesn't change her mind about telling us who is behind ASOME in the meantime," Rochelle added.

CHAPTER three

U-pon entering Monster High's main hall, Robecca, Rochelle, and Venus were greeted by throngs of students leaning limply against the green walls and pink coffin-shaped lockers. Above them in the rafters, clusters of sleeping bats dozed, blissfully unaware of the bedlam below. Directly ahead, rising from the well-polished purple-checkered floor, was a tombstone-shaped sign reminding students that it was against school policy to howl, molt fur, bolt limbs, or wake sleeping bats in the hallways.

Breezing past their slumped yet still wild-eyed peers, Robecca, Rochelle, and Venus scanned the hall for Wydowna. But there was neither sight nor sound of the spider ghoul.

"Where is she? I mean, she has six arms and bright red hair, she shouldn't be that hard to spot," Venus huffed as the trio neared the gym.

"Wydowna was pulled away by a very fast-moving crowd. So it's possible she's already inside," Rochelle stated, and then furrowed her brow. "Or at least that's what I'm hoping."

"We were so close. If only those vampires hadn't come," Robecca said as she stomped one of her copper boots against the floor.

"Robecca," a soft voice called out from a dimly lit corner of the hall.

"Cy!" Robecca replied as she threw up her arms in preparation for a hug.

"I've been looking everywhere for you. I was worried you might have been dinged or dented with everyone running around as if the normies were about to invade," Cy said after giving Robecca a quick pat on the back.

"Is that supposed to be a joke, Cy?" Venus said with a wry smile as she motioned for him to join them in the gym.

"That was the idea, but as you know Cyclopes are not well regarded for either their depth perception or their humor," the shy boy said while sneaking glances at Robecca.

"Holy hydrocarbons, am I glad to see your eye in one piece. With everyone charging across the field, I was sure you'd have a twig or rock lodged in there by now."

"I can't believe how worked up everyone got by the siren and code dead. But then again, if I actually believed the normies were threatening to wall us in, I guess I would be on edge too," the one-eyed boy muttered.

"Cy, you will be pleased to hear that we have convinced Wydowna to tell us who is behind ASOME," Rochelle said as she nervously clicked her hard claws together. "But, of course, we have to find her first."

Cy, Robecca, Rochelle, and Venus entered the gym and immediately began scanning the monsters huddled together on the Casketball court for any sign of Wydowna.

"I don't even like shutting my bedroom door. How am I going to live behind a wall? I need to be free to swim in the sea. A landlocked sea monster is like a hairless werewolf or a vegetarian vampire," sea creature Lagoona Blue groaned to her sometime boyfriend, freshwater-loving Gil Webber.

"Hey, what's wrong with being a vegetarian vampire?" Draculaura asked.

"Nothing, mate. Sorry, bad example," Lagoona said as she shook her head, realizing that she had just put her flipper in her mouth.

As the ghoulfriends walked past Lagoona, Gil, and Draculaura, a light drizzle fell upon them. This was a sure sign that Monster High's temporary headmistress, Miss Sue Nami, was near.

"Clear the way, non-adult entities," the water-logged woman bayed as she stomped toward Super-intendent Petra in the middle of the Casketball court. "What is happening in here, ma'am?"

"I am your superior. Therefore, informalities

such as 'ma'am' are not appropriate," Superintendent Petra grumbled, and then picked up her bullhorn. "Students are to form a single-file line," she continued as Salem's scariff, zombie Fred Onarrival, entered the room.

After offering the scariff a deferential nod of the head, Superintendent Petra watched as the student body formed one long and snaking line across the Casketball court.

"Students are to count off one by one, starting with you," Superintendent Petra announced into a bullhorn as Cy, Robecca, Rochelle, and Venus continued to crane their necks in search of Wydowna.

"*Could it be you're talking to me?*" a pumpkin head sang nervously as Superintendent Petra pointed at the small-bodied creature, whose normally pristine jack-o'-lantern was scuffed, no doubt a result of the stampede to get inside.

"I don't take kindly to interruptions, creature," Superintendent Petra said icily, and then once again signaled for him to count off.

"One," the pumpkin head chirped feebly while hugging his pet bullfrog tightly.

It was an odd thing, but most pumpkin heads at Monster High had bullfrogs, as they were both low-maintenance pets and natural metronomes.

"Why is *it* number one?" werecat Toralei purred, and then twitched her ears.

Dressed in white knee-high socks, wedge sneakers, and a studded dress, Toralei's ensemble was rather impractical for Crack and Shield Day.

"It?" the young pumpkin head mumbled under his breath, clearly taken aback by Toralei's description of him.

"I think we can all agree that the number one spot is permanently taken by me," the werecat continued as she tugged at Cleo's arm, which was intertwined with her own.

The school's biggest divas had taken to interlocking their arms as a security measure to ward off possible normie kidnappers. The peculiar idea had taken hold after Headmistress Bloodgood disappeared and Cleo's father, Ramses de Nile, worried that his daughter might be targeted by monarchy-obsessed normies. And so it came to be that Cleo and Toralei traveled in tandem, the idea being that two ghouls were infinitely more difficult to kidnap than one.

"Excuse me, Toralei Stripe?" Superintendent Petra said slowly, drawing out each word to display her aggravation at the interruption.

"Yeah, excuse me?" Cleo echoed, but for very different reasons.

"I'll handle this," Miss Sue Nami informed Superintendent Petra, and then turned to Toralei. "Non-adult entity known as Toralei Stripe, unless you want a permanent fur ball lodged in your throat, I suggest you can the small talk and count!"

"Two," Toralei said with a huff, and then rolled her eyes.

"Three," Cleo said as she adjusted her blue gauze-and-rhinestone tracksuit.

"Four," Frankie mumbled as she played nervously with her striped ponytail.

And so the numbers continued: five, twenty-eight, one hundred, and so on.

"Three hundred and one," Robecca said as steam billowed from both her nose and ears.

There was still no sign of Wydowna Spider anywhere.

"Three hundred and two," Rochelle said in a decidedly somber manner.

"Three hundred and three," Venus said as her vines stiffened with tension.

And then, as Superintendent Petra came to the last student in line, a small glint of joy appeared in her eyes.

"Three hundred and twenty-nine," a young vampire grumbled from the corner of the gym.

"Excellent. No one is missing," Superintendent Petra stated proudly as she checked something off on her clipboard.

"Actually, I think you've forgotten that the school recently added a new non-adult entity. Remember the ghoul we found in the attic?" Miss Sue Nami reminded

Superintendent Petra as delicately as possible.

"Wydowna Spider, if you are in here, please raise one of your six hands," Scariff Fred announced while scanning the crowd for the new ghoul. "By the looks of it, Petra, she's not here," he concluded.

"Why can't we ever catch a break?" Venus groaned, and then nervously began wringing her green hands together.

"Maybe she stopped by the Creepateria for a snack?" Robecca suggested hopefully.

"While it is possible, it is not probable," Rochelle replied as she shook her head at how close they had come to finding out the truth.

"No ghoul with lots of arms! No spider here!" a troll grunted as he waddled toward Miss Sue Nami, his long greasy locks swaying side to side.

"A missing non-adult entity is not good,"

Miss Sue Nami barked, and then turned toward Superintendent Petra. "Now might be a good time to tell me why you set off the alarm and dragged us all in here. Because if there is a new problem out there, I need to know about it."

"Miss Sue Nami, do not rush me," Superintendent Petra snapped haughtily.

"That was not my intention, ma'am. I am just worried about the ghoul, that's all," Miss Sue Nami explained.

"What did I tell you about calling me 'ma'am'?" Superintendent Petra snapped.

"Ma'am, I apologize."

"You just did it again!"

"Yes, I did, and I apologize again. It is how I addressed Headmistress Bloodgood and therefore is very hard for me to stop using," Miss Sue Nami clarified.

"Well, try."

"Yes, ma'am . . . ugh . . . I mean," Miss Sue Nami stuttered.

"Oh, forget it! I don't have time for this!" Superintendent Petra groused.

"I'm going to get my men to check the grounds for Wydowna. She might have gotten turned around. She is new, after all," Scariff Fred informed Superintendent Petra, and then walked off the court.

"Of all the ghouls to get lost," Robecca said, shaking her head.

"Vell, at least ve can sleep in her room vithout being voken up," Rose Van Sangre said to her twin sister, Blanche.

"Just vhat ve need, a good nap."

"Per the school's boarding policy, students are only to sleep in their assigned room," Rochelle stated authoritatively to the gypsy vampire twins.

"Don't waste your breath, Rochelle. Those two never listen. But on the bright side, at least they won't be loitering in our room tonight," Venus said, before releasing a long sigh.

"Per paragraph 5.8 of the Gargoyle Code of Ethics, I must inform others of misconceptions. Venus, there is no such thing as a wasted breath, for every breath keeps us alive. Except, of course, if you are a ghost, then it's a bit more complicated," Rochelle said as Scariff Fred reentered with a stressed expression.

"Wydowna Spider is nowhere to be found," he yelled into his special bullhorn, which translated his words from Zombese into English, just to make sure *everyone* could understand him.

"Maybe she ran away? After all, it was clearer than a ghost on a sunny day that she was not

Monster High material," Toralei piped up.

"And like my aunty Neferia says, with six arms spiders are always up to something," Cleo added.

"You two are like a leaf blower on a windy day," Venus grumbled at Toralei and Cleo.

"Is that some sort of recycling joke?" Toralei asked, narrowing her eyes at Venus.

"Definitely not the sharpest claw on the cat," Robecca mumbled under her breath.

"Excuse me, Scariff, but are you sure she isn't hiding in one of the classrooms? Or in her dorm room? Or in the attic?" Cy asked.

"We've searched every inch of this campus and she's not here. Now, she might have simply run away. But in light of Headmistress Bloodgood's kidnapping, we are obviously concerned. Perhaps the normies have raised the stakes and taken another monster to show us that they're serious about erecting the wall."

"Oh, they're serious all right; that's why I sounded the alarm," Superintendent Petra stated ominously. "One of our most trusted parents just returned from visiting with the normie sheriff, and you won't believe what he saw. . . ."

"What did this parent see, ma'am?" Miss Sue Nami questioned Superintendent Petra as the entire crowd listened with bated breath.

"He saw blueprints for the wall and a copy of the Monster High Fearbook with certain faces circled," Superintendent Petra explained.

"This parent believes that the circled pictures are kidnapping targets," Scariff Fred added.

"So for the time being, outdoor activities should be kept to an absolute minimum," Superintendent Petra stated emphatically to the room.

"*Excusez-moi*? But might we see this Fearbook? To confirm that Wydowna was circled?" Rochelle inquired politely.

"And who was the parent who went to see the normie sheriff?" Venus jumped in before Superintendent Petra had a chance to respond to Rochelle.

"Children, I do not like your tone. Not one bit. And we will not be telling you the monster's name, as we do not wish for him to be inundated with questions like why he wasn't able to take the Fearbook."

"Maybe someone ought to go to this normie sheriff's office and get a look at this Fearbook," Robecca blurted, and then remembered that there couldn't *be* a Fearbook to look at because she *knew* the normies were not actually behind any of this.

"Non-adult entity, I think that is a fine plan," Miss Sue Nami concurred, and then offered a sly wink at Robecca.

"I do not take kindly to an inferior, especially a soggy one, attempting to tell me what to do," Superintendent Petra shot back.

"With all due respect, ma'am, I would rather be soggy and wrinkly than so immutable that my expression for sheer terror and happiness are the same," Miss Sue Nami said as she approached Petra slowly.

"Petra versus the Nami, this is better than sliced-up salami," a few pumpkin heads sang as they watched the two forces of nature strut dramatically toward each other.

"What do they think this is? A duel in the Wild West?" Venus muttered.

"Those two are like oil and water—they just don't mix," Cy said as he shook his head at the ridiculous scene.

"Superintendent Petra? Miss Sue Nami? I'm sure I need not remind you that the entire student body is watching you both," Miss Flapper said in her usual soft and angelic manner. "Therefore, I think it wise that each of you go to opposite sides of the room and clear your heads."

"I never thought I would say this, but I actually agree with Madame Flapper. That was very sound advice," Rochelle whispered to her friends.

"And as far as this idea about taking the Fearbook from the normie sheriff, I think it's far too risky. It could inflame the normies, prompting them to do heaven knows what next. Plus, Wydowna was very lonely. Perhaps she left on her own," Miss Flapper suggested, standing between her loyal followers, Fanghai dragon Jinafire Long and Hexican *calaca* Skelita Calaveras.

"Of course she'd say that! She doesn't want anyone looking for her! That woman is like root rot to my soul," Venus moaned.

"Ma'am, since we are trying to stay inside, I suggest we return to our regular class schedule. For as you know, we ought to maintain as normal an environment for the students as we can," Miss Sue Nami said in a decidedly calmer manner than before. "We will, however, continue to turn over every stone looking for our lost student."

"I'm sorry, Miss Sue Nami, but I simply will not be able to return to work today. All that running and screaming was too much for me. You must remember that being dead is already very tiring, not to mention being me *and* being dead," Mr. D'eath lamented, before releasing a long and labored sigh.

"Okay, non-adult entities, back to your regularly scheduled classes," Miss Sue Nami ordered the crowd.

"I need to get to the Mad and Deranged Scientist Lab ASAP! Clearly, I'm going to have to learn how to make my own high-gloss hair products," Clawdeen fretted as she walked away, running her claws through her shiny brown locks.

"So this is it? We're just accepting the fact that the normies are going to lock us up?" Skelita asked the room as Miss Flapper nodded.

"How to handle the normies is a discussion for another time," Superintendent Petra snapped angrily at Skelita.

The static-faced woman then stomped out of the gymnasium, bringing the discussion to a close.

CHAPTER four

the spice-laden aroma of kung pao critters greeted Robecca, Rochelle, and Venus as they entered the Creepateria for dinner.

"Kung pao critters! Finally, something goes my way today. I love Fanghai cuisine," Venus remarked with excitement.

"While I too enjoy kung pao critters, I hardly think that this is something to rejoice over. After all, we still need to figure out who is behind ASOME. Once we do that we'll be able to not only expose the normie threat for what it is—a ruse to control and manipulate us—but also find Headmistress Bloodgood and Wydowna," Rochelle stated confidently as the trio sat down at a table.

"Way to burst my bubble," Venus grumbled under her breath.

"I did no such thing. How could I? There isn't *une bulle*, or bubble as you say, in sight," Rochelle countered.

"Remember the list of names we found hidden under the floorboard in the attic," Venus prompted her friends.

"Yeah, what about it?" Robecca responded.

"Do you ghouls think that list could be the monsters behind this secret group?" Venus suggested with some dread.

"Talk about a flea's sneeze, Venus! My father was

on that list! You couldn't possibly think my father, who has been missing for a century, could have something to do with this horrible group trying to ruin Monster High!" Robecca blubbered as steam poured out of her ears.

"No, no, of course not," Venus backed off quickly. "I forgot your father and Headmistress Bloodgood were on the list. There's no way either of them would be involved with something sinister."

"*Chérie*," Rochelle replied as she placed her hand on top of Robecca's. "Of course your father is not involved with this group. From a strictly logical perspective, it doesn't add up. Mr. Mummy said he had only ever heard rumblings of a secret society that believed in a monster hierarchy in the Old World. All the people on that list live in the Boo World."

"But what was the list for? And why were Headmistress Bloodgood's and your father's names circled?" Venus asked rhetorically as she lifted a huge forkful of kung pao critters to her mouth.

"I don't know. And do you know what else I don't know? Where is Penny? Grinding gears! Penny is going to be so grumpy! You know how she gets when I forget her somewhere!" Robecca fretted as she jumped up from the table with concern over her mechanical pet penguin.

"*Asseyez-vous*, sit down. Penny is most likely swatting away Venus's poor-sighted but always-hungry plant as we speak," Rochelle explained with a smirk. "That is to say, she's in our room with Roux and Chewy."

"Thank heavens! I was about ready to grind my gears. I just couldn't take facing a grumpy penguin after the day we've had," Robecca exclaimed, and then sighed with relief.

Later that evening, long past midnight, the sky turned a deep and magical purple. Not that any of the students at Monster High saw it, as they had all long since fallen asleep. But it was beneath this purple sky that a most peculiar thing transpired.

As Robecca, Rochelle, and Venus lay in bed fast asleep, they dreamed of everything from rust removal oils to couture clothing to wildflowers. And in their dreams, they each had a visitor. And though she looked different in each of their dreams, it was definitely Wydowna Spider. Her presence was a reminder that somewhere out there was a ghoul who needed their help. A ghoul who got caught up with the wrong people and was manipulated to do things that she didn't believe in. A ghoul who wanted to do the right thing. A ghoul whose only chance now lay in their green, granite, and copper hands.

Hours later, as the sun rose over the conifur trees at the edge of campus, yet another odd thing occurred. Rochelle popped out of bed, sure that it was time to get up. This was, of course, the usual domain of the chronically time-challenged Robecca. But on this morning it was Rochelle who sat straight up in bed, bright-eyed and ready to conquer the day. So you can imagine her surprise when she looked at the clock and saw that she had woken up two hours

52

early. It was then that she started thinking about Wydowna. And though she didn't remember her dream from the night before she felt a greater sense of duty to try and find the ghoul.

"Wake up, ghoulfriends! *Réveillez-vous!* I have an idea! A way to find Wydowna!" Rochelle proclaimed excitedly as she jumped out of bed.

Roux, ever the happy pet, leaped onto the floor and started running in circles around Rochelle's dainty gray feet. Roux was a delightful little creature who never failed to bring a smile to Rochelle's face.

"Robecca! Venus! *Réveillez-vous!* Did you hear me? I said wake up. We have work to do," Rochelle stated authoritatively. "And, per paragraph 4.7 of the Gargoyle Code of Ethics, one mustn't wait to help another."

"Huh," Venus moaned semi-lucidly from beneath her straw sleep mask, surrounded by a tangled mess of green and pink hair. "I just had the strangest dream about Wydowna."

"What? You're making my gears rattle!" Robecca yelped as she sat up in bed. "I dreamed about Wydowna too. And get this? She only had three arms in my dream. It was such a strange sight, two on the left and one on the right. I've got to admit, it looked pretty weird. Limbs definitely look better in sets, you know?"

"Can we talk about this later?" Venus mumbled as she turned over in bed.

Feeling impatient, Rochelle walked over to Venus, pulled back her eye mask, and stared the sleepy ghoul in the eye.

"Venus, I have an idea about how to find

54

Wydowna, but we must act quickly or the trail will disappear!" Rochelle explained animatedly.

"Let's do it! We need to find her! And not just because she deserves to be found but because she could really help us with this secret group ASOME," Robecca said as she jumped out of bed, much to the chagrin of the perennially sour-faced Penny.

"*Merci boo-coup*, Robecca. At least someone is responding appropriately this morning," Rochelle said, before shooting Venus an icy stare.

"So what's the plan, Stan?" Robecca asked, and then paused to clarify, "And yes, I know your name is not actually Stan."

"No, it is not, although I do have a very close friend in Scaris named Stan. He's president of the Student League of Rules and Regulations," Rochelle said proudly. "I must admit I've always been quite jealous of his position."

"Gargoyles and their rules . . . I just don't get it," Venus mumbled under her breath.

"Now then, back to Wydowna. Do you remember the scary tale about the brother and sister who left a trail of bread crumbs in the forest so that they could find their way back?" Rochelle asked her friends.

"Why are we talking about scary tales at six AM?" Venus huffed.

"Because what if Wydowna did that with her webbing? What if she left silky strands behind so that we could find where they are keeping her?" Rochelle suggested, her eyes gleaming with excitement.

Venus instantly bolted up in bed and threw back her gauze sheets.

"We need to move quickly. The more time that

passes, the more likely the strands are to either blow away or disintegrate," Venus responded seriously.

"But how do we know Wydowna is still somewhere on campus?" Robecca asked.

"We don't. They could have taken her anywhere. But considering how quickly she disappeared, I'm guessing she's somewhere close by, maybe even the same place where they're keeping Headmistress Bloodgood," Venus hypothesized as she pulled clothes on over her pajamas.

"While I agree that time is of the essence, surely there is enough time for us to properly change and brush our teeth," Rochelle asserted as she shook her head at Venus. "You know what the Gargoyle Code of Ethics says. . . ."

"No, but we're pretty sure you're going to tell us," Robecca offered with a smile.

Once they were washed up and changed, the trio tiptoed along the dormitory corridor, past the webbed curtain, and down the creaky rot-iron staircase into the main hall. From there they quickly exited the building and headed straight to the backfield.

"Okay, so Wydowna was about here the last time we saw her," Venus said while standing in the center of the lawn.

"And the vampires were headed up to school," Rochelle interjected.

"Which means they probably followed the main path," Robecca added as she started across the field.

"I don't see any strands yet," Venus mumbled while keeping her eyes trained on the ground, "although considering how many monsters stormed across the field after her, that's hardly a surprise."

Robecca, Rochelle, and Venus moved slowly across the lawn and up the path, scavenging for even the faintest sliver of webbing. But alas, they didn't find any.

"We mustn't lose hope yet. They might not have grabbed Wydowna until she was inside the main hall," Robecca reassured the others.

After a quick stop back in their room, the trio began their indoor search in the Mad and Deranged Scientist Laboratory, then moved on to the Study Howl, Libury, and catacombs. However, the only strands they came across were covered in dust.

"*S'il ghoul plaît*, Venus! Do not let Chewy eat that harmonica," Rochelle warned her friend, and then continued scanning the music room for spider webs.

"Chewy! No instruments! What did I tell you? You could only come if you didn't eat anything . . . or anyone," Venus reprimanded her plant playfully.

"I still do not understand why you two insisted on going back to the Chamber of Gore and Lore to get the pets," Rochelle said as she shook her head.

"Gee whiz, Rochelle, pets like to be included. I mean, just look at Roux, she's super happy to be here," Robecca replied.

"Yeah, but Roux is always happy. She even smiles when Chewy mistakes her for a piece of roast beast," Venus remarked.

"Speaking of food, we might as well head to the

Creepateria now for breakfast. *Évidemment*, my idea was a failure," Rochelle stated solemnly as she led the way down the hall.

After they sat down at a table, she continued, "*Je suis très désolée*, ghoulfriends. I got you up early for nothing, *absolument rien*."

"Jeepers, Rochelle, you have nothing to apologize for. It was a very good idea, and as my father always used to say, you never know until you try."

"*Merci boo-coup*, Robecca," Rochelle replied, and then grabbed hold of her left leg. "Stop it, Chewy!"

"What do you mean? Chewy's over here," Venus explained from across the table.

"Then it must have been Penny!"

"No, Penny's sitting on my lap," Robecca replied as the penguin whirred happily.

"Roux?" Rochelle wondered aloud, before spotting her pet griffin nearby. "No, she's over there running in circles, which means that it wasn't one of the pets who bit my leg."

Rochelle then slowly peered beneath the table and gasped.

"Vhat is the matter with you ghouls? Putting your feet all over us vhile ve are sleeping! Vhat, vere you raised in a barn?" the ghouls' dormmate Rose Van Sangre grunted groggily.

"A barn? Gargoyles do not live in barns. Don't you remember learning about gargoyles' natural habitats in class? If not, I suggest a summer revision. And, for your information, even animals in barns are raised not to bite one another."

"Vhy do they never let us sleep?" Blanche moaned dramatically while rolling her eyes.

"Maybe it has something to do with the fact that you two insist on sleeping in public," Robecca pointed out.

"You know vhat? I'm going zo go zo zhe town hall meeting and demand zey pass a sleep anyvhere law!" Blanche raved as she banged her pale fist against the underside of the table.

"What town hall meeting?" Venus interrupted.

"Zhe one zo zalk about how zo handle the normie problem. Or haven't zou heard? Zey're trying to vall us in."

CHAPTER five

s soon as Miss Sue Nami and Mr. D'eath arrived at the Creepateria for breakfast, Robecca, Rochelle, and Venus confirmed with them what the Van Sangre sisters had claimed. There was, in fact, a town hall meeting planned for the following day to address the "normie situation." Scariff Fred and Superintendent Petra had organized the event to review Salem's options and to put the word out about Wydowna's disappearance.

"I can't wait to hear what these so-called options are," Venus replied to Miss Sue Nami and Mr. D'eath sarcastically.

"Non-adult entity, you will not be hearing any such thing. Scariff Fred and Superintendent Petra have limited attendance to adults only," Miss Sue Nami snapped.

"That makes sense to me. After all, this is a pretty adult issue. It's the end of life as we know it, not that I technically have a life since I'm dead," Mr. D'eath moaned, and then wandered off without so much as a wave good-bye.

"We need to find him another date," Rochelle mused thoughtfully about their guidance counselor.

"Miss Sue Nami, we need to be at that meeting," Venus implored the acting headmistress.

"Listen up, non-adult entity, and listen up good,

because I don't like to repeat myself, especially when I'm hungry," she stated firmly, before breaking into her infamous body shake, sending water flying every which way.

"I must say I am most grateful for my water-resistant skin at this moment," Rochelle said as she watched the droplets roll right off her arm.

"Does anyone have a napkin? As you know, I'm absolutely terrified of rust, so I like to dry myself off immediately," Robecca said as she surveyed the many water spots on her arms and legs.

"Here you go, *chérie*," Rochelle said as she handed her friend a Scaremès scarf.

"Ghouls? Let's at least try to stay on track here," Venus blustered at her friends, and then turned back to Miss Sue Nami.

"There is no way I can allow you three non-adult

entities to attend. While I trust you all implicitly and I recognize how much you have done to protect Monster High, my current relationship with Superintendent Petra is too precarious to take any chances. If she found out that I let you three in, she'd throw me to the curb."

"To the curb? Why the curb?" Rochelle inquired genuinely.

"It's just a saying, Rochelle. She means Superintendent Petra would fire her," Robecca explained as she continued to dab the wet spots on her arms.

"Well, we certainly cannot allow that to happen. We've already lost one headmistress, we're not about to lose another!" Rochelle proclaimed steadfastly.

"With tough times we all need to make sacrifices. Do you think I wanted to cancel Career Day? No, but

I had to . . ." Miss Sue Nami trailed off as she focused on a passing monster. "Hey, non-adult werewolf? Yeah, I'm talking to you. Eating while walking is against the rules. So sit down. And brush your fur while you're at it. You look like something a werecat coughed up."

And with that the damp dame stomped off, knocking over both a chair and a pumpkin head in the process.

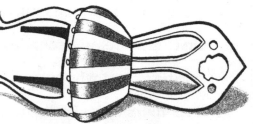

"I don't care what Miss Sue Nami said, we're not missing that meeting. It's too important," Venus whispered conspiratorially to Robecca and Rochelle.

"But it is against the rules!" Rochelle countered.

"Haven't you ever heard that some rules are meant to be broken?" Venus quipped.

"Yes, of course I have. It's called anarchy, chaos, lawlessness—" Rochelle pontificated.

"Pistons and pinecones, Rochelle! We aren't starting a revolution! We're just trying to help our school, and the monsters of Salem," Robecca explained simply.

"*D'accord*, okay, since this act could possibly help the greater good, I suppose I could make an exception. But that still doesn't change the fact that we are endangering Madame Sue Nami's position. And who knows what could happen with Superintendent Petra in charge?" Rochelle said, shaking her head, "*C'est trop dangereux*! It's just too dangerous to risk it!"

"We're going to *have* to risk it," Venus stated assuredly.

"I have never been very fond of that term

'risk it.' Gargoyles are notoriously risk averse."

"Look, I'm not trying to be a thorn in your side, but we don't have the luxury of missing this meeting. We're the only ones working to expose the truth!" Venus explained.

"She's right. Scariff Fred and Superintendent Petra wholeheartedly believe that the normies are doing this. It seems almost everyone does," Robecca said as steam billowed out of her small copper-plated ears.

"Very well. We will just have to be as discreet as possible. Do everything in our power to avoid detection. *Voler sous le radar*, fly under the radar," Rochelle acquiesced.

"Maybe we should disguise ourselves? You know, with wigs and masks and stuff. It will be like a secret mission and a costume party in one!" Robecca

71

suggested as her eyes widened with excitement.

"I don't think we have time to create believable costumes. It's well known in Scaris that a poor costume is worse than no costume at all."

"Maybe you're right. Plus, I didn't do so well that time we dressed up as werewolves at the Dance of the Delightfully Dead," Robecca remembered.

"No costumes. We'll just have to figure out another way into the meeting," Venus said as she fiddled with her vines.

After a long day of classes, including Ms. Kinder-grubber's lesson on how to make frozen yowlgurt, the trio headed to the Arts and Bats room for a Frightingale Society meeting.

Seated smack-dab in the middle of the room, the trio were surprised by just how dire the mood at Monster High had become. Long gone were the toothy smiles, bright eyes, and flowing hair, having been replaced with furrowed brows, frowns, and limp locks. Without faith in the future, the students of Monster High had fallen into a state of hopelessness, and it showed.

The copresidents of the Frightingale Society, Draculaura and Frankie, stood as they always did at the front of the room to address their fellow club members.

"A lot has changed at Monster High. We no longer

have Headmistress Bloodgood to watch over us. We no longer have the freedom to play outside or walk to school alone," Draculaura said as she fidgeted with one of her pink-and-black pigtails. "But that doesn't mean we should just give up and stop going to our classes—"

"And we understand that it's super hard to find the motivation to do homework when you feel like the future is darker than a blackout. But we must continue to care about our education. We must continue to learn. . . . It's who we are," Frankie said halfheartedly as though she were trying to convince herself as much as the others.

"Mates, I get what you're saying. I really do. But it's harder than catching a wave in Clawaii to study with this riptide of normies messing with our heads," Lagoona stated forlornly.

"If we let them change who we are, how we live, or our faith in the future, then they've already won," Frankie responded.

"Ghouls, Toralei is going to say something now," Toralei announced to the room as she stood up, pulling Cleo along with her.

"Did she just announce herself in the third person?" Robecca whispered to Venus.

"Are you surprised?" Venus said while shaking her head.

"Monsters are, like, totally claw-some," Toralei stated as though this were some kind of revelation, "so we need to be über strong and protect ourselves from outsiders, whether it's the normies or that thing from the attic."

"Wydowna is not a thing," Frankie corrected Toralei. "She's a spider ghoul."

75

"Eww! What is that? Do you have fleas?" Cleo suddenly screeched as she pointed at a small black thing on Toralei's arm.

"Has your brain been mummified or are you just blind? It's a piece of lint!" Toralei screamed.

"Ghouls, I simply cannot believe what I am hearing. *C'est incroyable*," Rochelle said as she stood up, paused to adjust the Scaremès scarf tied in her hair, and then continued. "It's not right! As a matter of fact, it's absolutely horrible!"

"This is, like, super weird, but I actually agree with the garg," Toralei drawled as she lifted her eyebrows to convey her surprise.

"First of all, no one shortens 'gargoyle' to 'garg,' as it does not sound very *agreeable*. And as for the other thing, I was actually referring to you, Toralei," Rochelle informed the werecat.

"Me? What about me? How *furr*ociously fabulous I am?"

"No, I was referring to what you said about Wydowna."

"Why must you say that clawful name in my presence? Just hearing it makes me feel like a vampire with a tan, if you know what I mean," Toralei expounded nonsensically.

"I am afraid I most definitely do not know what you mean," Rochelle shot back in her usual literal manner.

"Hearing her name is wrong, just like a vampire having a tan is wrong. And just so you know, I think it's super creepy that you are defending a ghoul who broke into our school and eavesdropped on us," Toralei snapped.

"First of all, vampires are incapable of tanning.

They only have two options, extremely pale or extremely burned. Second of all, your intense dislike of Wydowna for having camped out in the attic is irrational," Rochelle replied calmly.

"I guess it's true what they say about gargs. They really do have rocks for brains," Toralei remarked to Cleo, and then twitched her ears.

"That is categorically false—"

"Ghouls, let's not fight with each other, there's enough going on as it is," Frankie interrupted Rochelle.

"What are we going to do? What's going to happen to us?" Cleo whimpered to no one in particular, resting her furrowed brow in her hands.

"Don't fret, Cleo, not all is lost. Scariff Fred is holding a town hall meeting tomorrow at the Crier's Club to try and find a solution," Draculaura said in an attempt to comfort the angst-ridden mummy.

Rochelle, Robecca, and Venus all looked at one another. Now they knew where the meeting was going to be held!

CHAPTER Six

oday's the day. The town hall meeting starts at five PM," Venus said as she gave Chewy his morning shower with the watering can.

"While I do not enjoy breaking the rules, I am very eager to sneak into this meeting. We need a lead. Something to help us find Wydowna and Headmistress Bloodgood. Something to show Salem that the normies are not the threat, that ASOME is the threat . . . not that we know who they are . . ." Rochelle muttered as she made her bed.

"We had better eat a big breakfast," Robecca suggested as she walked toward the door. "My father always said that an empty stomach leads to an empty brain."

Just as Robecca, Rochelle, and Venus exited their dorm room to head down to the Creepateria for breakfast, Jinafire Long appeared before them.

"*Zǎo ān*. Good morning, ghouls," the green-and-black-haired dragon said as her long gold tail flitted back and forth.

"Good morning, Jinafire," Robecca responded. "Is everything okay? You look a little fired up—no pun intended."

"While I am in complete control of my fire breath, things are most definitely not *okay*, as you say."

"What is it, Jinafire? Has something happened? Remember, I'm a gargoyle, I'm very good in times of trouble," Rochelle said as she reached out and patted the dragon ghoul's gold arm.

"There is an old Fanghai proverb: In order to protect others, you must first protect yourself."

"It is the same principle that flight crews use: One must first put on his or her own oxygen mask before helping others with theirs," Rochelle said with a smile, clearly pleased to use her knowledge of aviation protocol.

"Yes, Rochelle," Jinafire responded, before looking each of the ghouls in the eye. "I would like to invite the three of you to come into my dorm room for a very important demonstration."

"Thanks for the invite, but we're super hungry. Can we take a rain check?" Venus asked as her stomach began to growl louder than a werewolf during a full moon.

"Venus, your stomach makes even more noise than my rusty joints," Robecca said with a giggle.

"This is no laughing matter, ghouls. So please follow me," Jinafire stated authoritatively.

"Venus, *chérie*, I do not like upsetting your stomach, but perhaps we should spare a few minutes for Jinafire's demonstration," Rochelle said as she started after the dragon.

"Never a dull moment at Monster High," Robecca mused as she grabbed hold of Venus's arm and followed Jinafire and Rochelle.

"Dragon kung boo is a very old and traditional martial art. One which my family has practiced for centuries," Jinafire informed Robecca, Rochelle, and Venus as the trio sat scattered around her and Skelita's dorm room.

Jinafire then draped herself in a long white robe

and tied it with a sash.

"Does everyone wear that outfit when practicing kung boo?" Robecca asked.

"It is called a *gi*. And no, not everyone. I find it comfortable."

"And that wasn't to imply that I don't like the way it looks, because I do. Not that it matters if your outfit is stylish when you are working out and sweating. I, of course, can't sweat. It's one of the few perks of being crafted out of a steam engine. Although now that I think about it, steaming is kind of like sweating, only without the odor. Heavens to batsy, what am I going on about? You must all think I am missing a few cogs!" Robecca rambled on.

"Statistically speaking, it is highly probable that you are missing a part or two. Very few creatures manage to be reassembled without losing a cog, screw, or spring in the process," Rochelle added in her usual literal manner.

Jinafire then began demonstrating several different moves before being interrupted by Venus.

"Why exactly did you choose today to invite us over for a self-defense lesson?" Venus asked.

"Actually," a soft voice floated into the room from the doorway, "it was my idea."

"Madame Flapper," Rochelle said after spotting the always-graceful European dragon.

Dressed in a long and flowing lavender jumpsuit with intricate lace details, Miss Flapper was as breathtakingly stylish as usual. However, it was not simply the woman's outfit that was capturing Rochelle's attention but the materials used to create the long lavender ensemble.

"The lace trim on your clothing is *très*

86

fangtastique. It takes incredible precision and skill to create something of that caliber. Surely this must be the work of Wydowna," Rochelle blurted out.

"Rochelle, Miss Flapper could have gotten that lace anywhere. After all, it's not like she even knew Wydowna that well, remember?" Venus stated pointedly.

"But it looks identical to some of the pieces Wydowna created," Rochelle continued, oblivious to Venus's attempt to shut down her line of questioning.

Unsure how else to communicate her message, Venus began elbowing Rochelle. But as so often happens, she stopped after remembering that granite and elbows proved a very painful combination.

"You have a very good eye, Rochelle. This is indeed the work of Wydowna Spider. I had it commissioned right before she fled Monster High. It really is a shame that such a talented ghoul couldn't make any friends here. But in the end, in light of the danger we're facing, maybe she's better off," Miss Flapper stated cautiously.

"Fled? Why do you think Wydowna fled? A lot of monsters are speculating that she was taken by the normies," Robecca inquired.

"Scariff Fred said that it was as likely that the ghoul ran away as it was that she was kidnapped. But think about it, they took Headmistress Bloodgood because they knew everyone would miss her. They tried to take me because, while not as well loved as the headmistress, I do have a few supporters," Miss Flapper said, before smiling at Skelita and Jinafire. "But why would they take a new spider ghoul, someone who had yet to make one friend at Monster High? She was still very much a stranger to our community. I think she was just homesick."

"I don't know about that," Robecca responded without thinking.

"What? I thought you had barely spoken to her," Miss Flapper pressed Robecca.

"Yep, that's right," Robecca declared nervously.

"Thanks for the kung boo lesson, Jinafire. It was really cool!" Venus exclaimed in a desperate attempt to change the subject.

"I do hope that the few simple moves that I taught you will help if you ever find yourself face-to-face with a kidnapper," Jinafire replied.

"Well, we better get going, we've got a big day today," Robecca uttered, once again without thinking.

"What do you mean? Are you referring to the town hall meeting? Because I was told that students weren't allowed to attend," Miss Flapper asked, all the while maintaining a taut smile.

"Students are most definitely not allowed at the meeting," Venus quickly answered. "Robecca was referring to Mr. Mummy's quiz in Catacombing class."

"Yes, that is exactly what I was referring to. Thank you, Venus," Robecca stated stiffly as steam dribbled out of her ears.

The town hall meeting at the Crier's Club was starting at five PM sharp. But as Robecca, Rochelle, and Venus did not wish any of the parents or teachers attending the meeting to see them, they waited until 4:40 PM to leave campus. With a short window of time in which to make it to the meeting, the trio cut through the grove of conifurs, dodged the trolls at the edge of campus, and then ran like crazy into town.

Upon arriving in Salem, the trio saw that things were far from normal. The once busy village was eerily empty save for the odd cat and dog roaming around. The Die-ner appeared abandoned, without so much as a waiter or busboy in sight. The Maul had a sign posted on the door stating that it was closed for the town hall meeting.

"Wow, it's like the apocalypse over here. There isn't a monster left," Venus said to Robecca and Rochelle as they turned onto Elm Street en route to the Crier's Club. "I know this is going to sound weird, but I find the emptiness kind of peaceful."

"Really? I can't stand it! It's giving me a serious case of the heebie-jeebies! Why, just look at me, my bolts are rattling!" Robecca babbled as her eyes darted from side to side in search of anything suspicious. "And even though I know for a fact that we have nothing to fear from the normies, I'm pretty on edge, like I'm waiting for one of them to jump out at me."

"*C'est absolument ridicule!* It is absolutely ridiculous! Normies do not jump out at people, unless, of course, you are playing hide-and-screech with them," Rochelle clarified.

"I agree, but what about another monster? Maybe someone from this secret organization ASOME? It's not totally impossible," Venus said as she motioned for the others to follow her onto Warren Street.

As the threesome turned the corner onto the tree-lined lane, they stopped dead in their tracks. Venus's vines prickled, Robecca's copper plates trembled, and Rochelle's wings fluttered as they took in the scene. Miss Flapper and Cy Clops walking together. And though the trio was at least thirty feet behind Cy and Miss Flapper, there was no mistaking either of them. Dressed in an emerald-green gown that beautifully complemented her long red hair and lithe silhouette, Miss Flapper gracefully floated along as only she could. And as for Cy, the evidence was equally hard to refute. The boy was sporting a bright purple backpack with his name embroidered on it.

"I don't believe my eyes," Venus mumbled as she shook her head. "Is that Cy with Miss Flapper?"

"You may rest assured that your eyes are not playing tricks on you. It is most definitely Cy and Madame Flapper," Rochelle stated unequivocally.

"Then I guess the question isn't whether my eyes are playing tricks on me but whether Cy is playing tricks on us," Venus postulated as she suspiciously raised her left eyebrow.

"Jeez Louise, Venus! He's our friend! Don't you think he deserves a chance to at least explain himself? Especially after everything we've been through with him."

"Robecca is *absolument correct*. Plus, paragraph 65.9 of the Gargoyle Code of Ethics states that one should not jump to conclusions based on circumstantial evidence. And this is most definitely circumstantial evidence."

"What is this, *Claw & Order*?" Venus said with a huff, before relenting. "Fine. You guys are right. It's just that seeing those two together really threw me for a loop."

"Quick!" Robecca yelped as she grabbed hold of both Rochelle's and Venus's arms and pulled them behind a parked car.

94

Crouched behind an old rusted truck, Robecca, Rochelle, and Venus craned their necks to see what Miss Flapper and Cy were doing.

"Sorry about that, ghouls. I thought she was about to turn around. And then I started worrying about what would come out of my mouth, because, as we all know, I'm not good on the spot or under pressure," Robecca muttered.

"Not to worry, *chérie*. A ghoul must always trust her instincts," Rochelle answered.

"Except, of course, when it comes to the time. Then you should never ever trust your instincts. Because if I have learned anything about you these past two semesters, it's that you haven't a clue what time it is," Venus added.

"They've stopped walking," Robecca noticed as Miss Flapper and Cy stood in front of the two-story brick building that housed the Crier's Club. "Now they're talking."

"Thanks for the narration," Venus joked as Miss Flapper patted Cy on the shoulder and then walked into the club.

"Miss Flapper has flown the coop," Robecca continued.

"Come on, ghouls," Venus instructed Rochelle and Robecca as she jumped up from behind the old truck and started running down the street.

But so eager was Robecca to talk to the one-eyed boy that she quickly jetted past Venus.

"Hey! Hey! Cy!" Robecca called out as she charged toward him with Venus and Rochelle close behind.

"Hey, ghouls. What's going on? What are you doing here?"

"How funny! That's just what we were about

to ask you," Venus said as she whipped her pink ponytail around and raised her eyebrows.

"Miss Flapper came to my dorm room and asked if Henry or I would walk her to the Crier's Club. She said she was worried about her safety," Cy repeated while shaking his head incredulously. "And since I thought she might say something helpful, I offered to accompany her."

"*S'il ghoul plaît*, Cy! I am not very good with anticipation. What did she say?" Rochelle squealed.

"She mostly talked about her clothes and how no one will ever fully understand how amazingly stylish she is—" Cy recalled.

"Clothes? That's it?" Venus interrupted.

"No, then right at the end she asked if I had seen Wydowna hanging out with anyone in particular while she was at Monster High."

"Madame Flapper is clearly worried that Wydowna might have told us something," Rochelle said as she began rubbing her chin.

"If only those vampires would have come a minute later, she might have actually told us something of use," Venus said with a sigh.

"It's almost five. The meeting is about to start," Rochelle informed the others.

"Venus, how did you say we were sneaking in again?" Robecca chimed in.

"You're sneaking into the meeting?" Cy repeated.

"As you know, I do not as a rule break rules. However, the Gargoyle Code of Ethics clearly states that rules may be broken when the results of said action will aid in the greater good, which clearly applies to this situation," Rochelle explained seriously.

"Then I'm coming with you ghouls," Cy responded.

98

"Great! We could always use another set of eyes and ears. Or rather eye and ears. Oh! You know what I mean," Robecca babbled as Venus started around the back of the building.

Hidden behind an assortment of trash cans was a metal ladder bolted to the wall.

"Isn't this *fangtastique*? Fire safety precautions are helpful even when there isn't a fire," Rochelle mused.

"So I guess this means we're going in via the roof," Robecca said. "Good thing none of us is afraid of heights."

"We're going to climb up to the roof, remove the air vent, and then jump down into the back stairwell, which leads to an internal balcony that overlooks the hall," Venus explained, before grabbing hold of the ladder.

"Have you been moonlighting at the Crier's Club?

How do you know the layout?" Robecca inquired.

"Lagoona and I entered into an investigation last semester after hearing that the manager had stopped recycling. But luckily, it turned out to be a false alarm."

"Jeepers, Venus! And you didn't tell us?"

"I didn't think the Code of Ethics would approve," Venus explained while motioning at Rochelle.

"You may be correct. I need more facts. However, as time is slipping away, discussion of your investigation is going to have to wait," Rochelle said, and then grabbed onto the ladder behind Venus.

Less than ten seconds had passed and already the metal bars were groaning and bolts were popping out of the wall.

"It's raining hardware," Robecca exclaimed as she raised her hands to shield Cy's large eye from the falling metal debris.

"The ladder's about to become completely unhinged from the wall!" Cy yelled at Rochelle and Venus.

"That just leaves us one choice, then—jump!" Venus instructed Rochelle.

The sound of the two ghouls crashing against the cement ground resulted in quite a thud, mostly due to Rochelle's sturdy granite composition.

"Ouch!" Venus moaned as she slowly stood up and dusted herself off.

"One of the good things about being crafted from stone is that it takes a lot to bruise me. However, the heavy nature of stone also means that I am rather prone to having items collapse beneath me," Rochelle mumbled quietly.

"It's no big deal, Rochelle," Venus said as she

looked around. "Except that now we need to find another way up to the roof."

"No problem; I've got that covered," Robecca said as she flipped the switch to her rocket boots and smiled. "Who wants to go first?"

"It sure does pay to have a ghoulfriend who can fly," Venus remarked, and then wrapped her arms around the copper-plated ghoul's waist.

Robecca seamlessly jetted Venus to the top of the building and then returned to get Rochelle and Cy.

"Are you certain you can lift me?" Rochelle questioned Robecca. "I might not look very heavy, but believe me, I am."

"Rocket boots are pretty powerful. So you don't need to worry about me," Robecca replied.

"*D'accord*," Rochelle said as she grabbed hold of Robecca and braced herself.

Much to the gargoyle's relief, the flight up went off without a hitch. And so after bringing Cy to the roof, the foursome managed to pry open an air vent and drop into the back stairwell. Immediately upon entering, the foursome heard the sound of monsters talking. And with each step they took, the voices grew louder and clearer.

"From here, we have to crawl," Venus whispered to the others as she got down on her hands and knees and started making her way across the balcony, which overlooked the large meeting hall.

Lying flat on the ground, the foursome discreetly peered down at the audience below. It was a full house, without even one empty chair. But then again, who would miss a meeting to discuss the future of their town? Just then, the faint sound of the bell tower striking five echoed through the large room.

CHAPTER Seven

"Would everyone please take a seat," Superintendent Petra announced as she and Scariff Fred walked to the podiums positioned at the front of the Crier's Club.

"In light of our current situation with the normies, we are turning to the community to help us find a possible solution. So with that in mind, I hereby call this town hall meeting in session," Scariff Fred said into a microphone.

As the crowd of concerned monsters exchanged nervous glances, as if to say "who's going to go first," an elderly pumpkin head stood up.

"Is it true that the normies plan to divide Salem into sections based on our age? Because I'm not fond of my peers, so the idea of being locked up with them is pretty awful," the man grumbled, and then sat back down.

"Unfortunately, sir, we have not been given any information as to their plans after the wall goes up," Scariff Fred responded.

"That's because the normies aren't planning anything," Robecca whispered to Cy as they lay on the floor of the balcony.

"As of now, all we can tell you is that the normies are planning on erecting the wall very soon. After which, they should return Headmistress Bloodgood and anyone else they might take in the meantime," Scariff Fred finished.

"I would like to take this moment to point out that I no longer allow any of Monster High's students to linger outside, so as to decrease their chances of being kidnapped. I also arranged for deputies to escort students during the morning and afternoon school runs," Superintendent Petra stated with pride and, of course, her usual blank expression.

"Superintendent Petra? While I commend your efforts to keep our cubs safe, I worry that we've gotten carried away without taking the time to fact-check our information," Clawdeen's father, Mr. Wolf, said as tactfully as possible.

"Fact-check our information? Mr. Wolf, this is an issue of local security, not some term paper on Gillary Clinton!" Superintendent Petra snapped.

"I didn't mean for it to come out like that," Mr. Wolf replied calmly. "I only meant that it would be helpful if we knew who your source was; as in, who visited the normie mayor?"

"The source is a trusted member of the monster community with a long-standing relationship with the normie mayor," Scariff Fred responded cryptically.

"Yes, but what's his or her name?" Mr. Wolf continued.

"I will not tell you his name, sir. Why should I? So he can be harassed day and night by a bunch of terrified monsters. Absolutely not!" Scariff Fred stated firmly.

"But—" Mr. Wolf started to respond, before being cut off by Superintendent Petra.

"I would encourage you to sit down, Mr. Wolf," the coldhearted mummy interjected.

Mr. Wolf returned to his seat just as Deuce's mother, Mrs. Gorgon, stood up.

"Scariff Fred, first I would like to thank you for all that you and your subordinates have been doing to keep us safe," Mrs. Gorgon said as she pushed one of the snakes slithering across her forehead back. "But I must ask, why did you shut the borders? Why have you stopped us from leaving Salem?"

"Where were you trying to go, Mrs. Gorgon?" Scariff Fred inquired.

"I wanted to speak with a few normies, to confirm that everything we are hearing is accurate," Mrs. Gorgon answered honestly.

"That is exactly why I closed the border. Who knows what could happen if you said the wrong thing? It's simply too dangerous to keep the borders open," Scariff Fred decreed.

"I think we are getting a bit off subject here," Superintendent Petra remarked. "The point of this meeting is to review our choices, if we have any, that is. . . ."

"We could all leave! A mass exodus!" a twentysomething vampire shouted from the left side of the hall.

"Let's find a more monster-friendly territory," a middle-aged sea creature cried out from the back of the room. "Preferably somewhere near the ocean!"

"Who knows? Maybe living in a walled-in community will be nice. Although no one will ever be able to visit us and we'll never be able to leave," a middle-aged dragon said as she began to tear up.

"What about the IMF?" a mummy called out.

"Unfortunately, the International Monster Federation does not have a military arm," Super-intendent Petra explained.

"Excuse me, excuse me?" Miss Flapper called out as she stood up and looked around at the crowd. "Hello, everyone. As most of you know, I haven't been in Salem long. But in the short time that I've lived here I've come to consider it home, even more so than Bitealy, where I used to teach. So I can't bear to see us lose our way of life, our town, our freedom. . . ."

"But what can we do?" a woman's voice shrieked from behind Miss Flapper.

"Back in the Old World, there were rumors of a powerful group of monsters, a secret society," Miss Flapper said slowly as a hush swept across the crowd. "And though I've never dealt with them personally, I heard from an old colleague that their mission is to protect monsters, our traditions, our core beliefs . . . at any cost.".

"When I lived in Transylvania, I heard similar rumblings about this group too. But how do you know they'd be willing to travel to the Boo World to help us?" a well-dressed mummy inquired.

"I've been told that ASOME, as they are called, is more than willing to come to the Boo World and help us," Miss Flapper answered.

"Excuse me! Excuse me!" Dracula hollered as he stormed to the front of the Crier's Club. "With all due respect to Miss Flapper, we don't know a thing about this ASOME group. They could be dangerous! Trust me; I'm from the Old World. The way they do things there is not necessarily how we should do things here!"

"Mr. Dracula, do you care for your daughter

Draculaura?" Miss Flapper questioned the dapperly dressed vampire.

"What kind of question is that? Of course I do," he huffed in response.

"Then why are you standing in the way of the only thing that could possibly save her future?" Miss Flapper asked solemnly.

"I don't think getting in with a group that we've only heard rumors about is very smart. There must be another way. And I suggest we find it! Now who is with me?" Dracula called out to the crowd.

First to stand up were the Wolfs; then Mrs. Gorgon; then Ghoulia's mother, Mrs. Yelps; and finally Frankie's father, Mr. Stein.

"It's all the monsters from the list we found in the attic! Well, except for Hexiciah Steam and

Headmistress Bloodgood, that is," Venus whispered excitedly to Rochelle.

"Shh!" Rochelle instructed Venus while putting a finger up to her lips.

One by one, Dracula, Mr. Stein, Mrs. Yelps, Mrs. Gorgon, and the Wolfs turned and stared at Ramses de Nile. But the mummy was so engaged in conversation with his sister Neferia that he did not react. It was not until his sibling, who was visiting from the Old World, nudged her brother that he noticed. But once he did, he quickly stood up in solidarity with the others.

"Jeepers, look at Mr. De Nile's sister. She looks about as nice as an ice pick in my gear box," Robecca mumbled.

"Is it just me or does Cleo's dad look annoyed about joining the others?" Venus whispered to Cy, Robecca, and Rochelle.

"While I agree that he does not look happy, I feel it is important to point out that he always looks like that. Smiling is not a high priority in the De Nile clan," Rochelle quietly responded.

"That's it? No one else is going to stand up against calling in ASOME?" Cy asked, and then sighed. "This is not a good sign."

Early the next morning, Rochelle and Venus woke as they often did to the sound of Robecca falling out of bed, absolutely sure that she was late.

"Cranking cogs! What time is it? What time is it? I'm late! I can feel it! I'm late!" Robecca babbled frantically as she pulled herself off the floor.

"Relax, Becs," Venus said from beneath her straw

eye mask. "You're not late. At least not right now. So go back to bed and we'll wake you when it's time to get up."

"You have no idea how stressful it is to never know the time. I would do anything to see my father again, and not just because I love and miss him, but so he could fix my broken internal clock."

"You will see him again . . . someday . . . somewhere," Rochelle responded softly, clearly still asleep. "And after you do, maybe then we'll all be able to sleep through the night without interruption."

It was not until lunchtime that day that news of the town hall meeting fully spread through Monster High, piquing the students' interest in ASOME. Understandably, news of a mysterious yet all-powerful group that could stop the wall garnered much attention.

"I don't know what happened at that meeting last night, but my parents were totally freaking out when they came home. It was crazy, even their fur looked stressed out," Clawdeen recalled to Frankie, Deuce, Robecca, Rochelle, and Venus over quiche gorelaine in the Creepateria. "So I asked them what happened and they were like, 'Nothing, nothing at all,' which means something definitely happened."

"Oh yeah, something *definitely* happened," Frankie stated unequivocally. "I heard my dad talking about how Miss Flapper brought up some clandestine organization from the Old World called ASOME. Apparently Miss Flapper claims they can help us fight the normies, but my dad says they are bad news."

"My mom thinks the same. She was so stressed out when she got back home last night that she turned three possums and a cat to stone. Those poor critters, they'll be like that for at least a week," Deuce lamented from behind his black sunglasses.

"Well, Rochelle, Venus, and I live in the dorm, so we didn't hear anything. Not a single thing. We literally don't have the faintest idea what happened at that meeting," Robecca added unnecessarily in a poor attempt to cover up the fact that the ghouls had attended the meeting.

"Becs, can you pass the salt?" Venus asked while

attempting to convey a very important message with her eyes—*stop talking*!

"*Regardez*! It's Cleo and Toralei, what a wonderful surprise," Rochelle proclaimed, eager to focus the table's attention on something new.

"Deuce, you're my boyfriend, right?" Cleo drawled, and then pursed her perfectly glossed lips together.

"Last time I checked," Deuce said with a chuckle.

"Then why didn't you wait for me to start lunch? Remember, I'm not just your ghoulfriend, I'm royalty. And everyone waits for royalty."

"Clearly, not everyone," Toralei muttered.

"Babe, I'm sorry to say this, but until you and Toralei work out your issues, I think it's best I keep my distance when food is involved," Deuce explained.

"What is that supposed to mean, snakebrain?" Toralei snapped.

"I don't mean any disrespect to either of you, it's just that last time you two threw ghoulash at each other, it landed on my head. And, well, ghoulash and snakes do not mix. These poor guys were sick for hours," Deuce said as he pointed to his Mohawk of snakes.

"Whatever. I'll be rid of you all soon enough," Toralei purred under her breath, and then twitched her ears.

"Why, are you going somewhere? I hear Sifearia is lovely this time of year," Venus chimed in.

"No, I just meant that once ASOME handles the normies, I won't have to be attached to this decomposing diva who always insists on dragging me over to see you lot."

"It's true, my dad and Aunty Neferia told me that ASOME is going to save us," Cleo seconded. "And for the last time, you fur ball, I am not a decomposing diva, just a posing diva."

"Fur ball? Is that the best you've got?"

"Of course not! Why would I give you the best that I've got?" Cleo retorted.

"Come on, you two, what do you say we head to the Libury and let these monsters eat in peace," Deuce said as he stood up from the table and smiled at Clawdeen, Frankie, Robecca, Rochelle, and Venus. "See you ghouls at Career Day."

"Madame Sue Nami? *S'il ghoul plaît*, we must speak with you!" Rochelle called out after the puddle-prone woman as she stormed down Monster High's main hall, taking out anyone who got in her way.

"If you want to speak with me, then walk faster! I'm on a schedule here!" Miss Sue Nami roared at the trio.

"A schedule?" Robecca repeated to herself. "I sure do hope that one day I can follow a schedule. . . ."

"Career Day is back on?" Venus questioned the acting headmistress after finally catching up with her.

"Your information is accurate, non-adult entity."

"But why the sudden change? As of yesterday you said that holding Career Day at such an uncertain time was a form of mental torture," Venus pressed on.

"Madame Sue Nami, might it have something

to do with this ASOME group everyone is talking about?" Rochelle asked.

"As a matter of fact, yes, it does. After learning about ASOME, I realized that the future might be a bit brighter than we previously thought."

"But no one knows that much about ASOME. Plus, if our sources are correct, wasn't it Miss Flapper who suggested it?" Venus inquired.

"Look, I don't think the normies are up to what everyone says they are, but the fact remains, I don't know what's happening here. And if there's a group of monsters out there that can calm everyone down and help them release their fears, then I'm on board. Bottom line, as of now I'm A-OK with ASOME," Miss Sue Nami declared loudly.

"Us too," Jinafire and Skelita piped up as they walked by Miss Sue Nami and the ghouls in the hall.

"You ghouls know about ASOME too?" Robecca wondered aloud.

"Miss Flapper told us that they're going to stop the wall. We are very *gǎnxiè* or grateful that they are willing to help their fellow monster," Jinafire explained.

"Plus, Senorita Flapper said she thinks they'll have killer couture clothes," Skelita squealed.

"I only wish ASOME had a booth at Career Day," Jinafire said, before continuing on to the event.

The gymnasium was teeming with booths, each dedicated to a different profession. There was the mad scientist, the coffin builder, the furrier, the talon scout, and countless others. And as Robecca and

Venus browsed the many booths, Rochelle stopped to ponder something in front of the formaldehyde expert.

"Everything okay back there?" Venus asked Rochelle.

"*Je ne crois pas*. I don't think so," Rochelle said cryptically as she rubbed her cold gray chin. "Something very peculiar happened at lunch."

"Did you find something in your quiche? That Harold in the Creepchen is always losing his claws in the food. It's the absolute flea's sneeze," Robecca said while shaking her head.

"That is a most disturbing fact regarding Harold, one which I will most definitely address at a later date. However, I was actually referring to what Cleo said. She claimed that her father told her that ASOME was going to save us from the normies.

But at the town hall meeting Ramses supported Dracula's motion to steer clear of the group," Rochelle explained as she continued to rub her chin. "It simply does not add up."

"You're right," Venus agreed. "Why would he tell her that if he doesn't actually believe it?"

"Well, speak of the devil! Not that he's actually the devil! It's just a saying! Oh, forget it, just look! It's Dracula!" Robecca said as she pointed toward his Never Fail, Always Pale sunscreen booth.

"Come on, let's see what information we can get out of him," Venus suggested as they started toward the booth.

"*Boo-jour*, Monsieur Dracula. I would like to commend you on your safety-conscious line of sunscreen. Even though I do not personally use sunscreen, as I am crafted out of granite, I am a very big proponent of it. Especially for those with sensitive skin, like Venus," Rochelle explained to the pale-faced man in a well-tailored black velvet suit.

"It's true that plants have very delicate skin. And while they need sunlight for photosynthesis, too much of it can cause wilting," Dracula explained, and then paused, unnerved by the intensity with which Venus, Robecca, and Rochelle were staring at him. "Um, this is one of my smaller companies, but it's profitable. Was there something else, ghouls? Having a little anxiety about planning your careers?"

"It's about ASOME," Rochelle blurted out.

"Must you always be so direct?" Venus muttered to her friend.

"Yes, paragraph 6.9 of the Gargoyle Code of Ethics states that being forthright in times of crises is paramount to escaping said times."

"Listen here, ghouls, you don't need to worry your pretty little heads about ASOME. The adults are handling things," Dracula stated in a less-than-convincing manner.

"While our heads are all very pretty, they most certainly are not little. As for the adults handling things, we both know that is not true. And just in case you have forgotten, our pretty little heads are the ones who stopped Madame Flapper's Whisper spell," Rochelle asserted powerfully.

"I'm sorry. I didn't mean to condescend or discredit what you ghouls have accomplished. I was just trying to calm your nerves. You *are* kids, after all," Dracula responded candidly.

"Here's the thing; it hasn't even been twenty-four hours since Miss Flapper brought up this ASOME idea and already everyone is talking about them like they're our saviors. So if you want to stop them, you better do something and fast," Venus replied.

CHAPTER eight

by the time the final bell of the day echoed through the corridors and classrooms of Monster High, ASOME fever had reached an absolute frenzy. Monsters walked faster, talked louder, and generally looked more alert as they delighted in the news.

"ASOME to save the day! Go to my blog for the latest on the secret organization set to rescue Monster High from the grasp of the normies!" pale-skinned ghost Spectra Vondergeist said as she floated down the hall, her chains rattling against her lavender lace-up boots.

"Hey you! Ghoul with the purple hair! No yelling in hall! That the rule!" a troll grunted in broken Fanglish at Spectra while waving his filthy finger in her face.

"I don't have time for rules. I'm too busy covering history. Or haven't you heard? ASOME is going to stop the normies from walling us in," Spectra replied with gusto as she continued gliding just above the purple-checkered floor.

"*Boo-la-la*! What a peculiar thing to say. Who doesn't have time for rules? Why, I've never even heard of such a thing," Rochelle babbled as she watched Spectra's purple locks disappear from view. "Rules are what keep society running! Rules are the cornerstone of civilization! Rules are—"

"Heavens to batsy, Rochelle! Who cares about rules?" Robecca interrupted.

"*Évidemment*, I do. That is why I said what I said," Rochelle replied directly.

"I'm getting worried," Venus said as she looked around the hall and noted the manic energy of her peers.

"Tell me about it. This growing obsession with ASOME is about to make me steam up—big time," Robecca declared as she furrowed her copper brow.

"It's definitely not good. But we did warn Dracula. Although I couldn't tell how seriously he took our warning," Venus responded.

"I believe Monsieur Dracula realizes that support for ASOME is increasing. However, I doubt he realizes just how fast it's growing. I must say, even I am a

133

bit surprised by it," Rochelle said as she noticed a vampire pinning a poster to the wall.

"A is for Awesome. S is for Savior. O is for Oppressing the normies. M is for Monster protectors. E is for Evil destroyers," Venus read the sign aloud. "Wow, that is some serious ASOME propaganda right there."

"And now for the musical version," Rochelle replied as she motioned to a pumpkin head skipping happily down the hall.

"ASOME is going to save Monster High! Now we can all relax and sigh! Thank you, Miss Flapper, for a happy ever after," the petite creature crooned as Cy approached the trio.

"Hey, ghouls, have you see Spectra's blog?" Cy asked while shaking his head. "I don't even know what to say."

"*Moi non plus*. Neither do I. But I mean that literally, as I have yet to read her blog," Rochelle explained to Cy.

"Spectra took a poll, and it turns out that ninety percent of Salem monsters and ninety-three percent of Monster High students support the idea of reaching out to ASOME to help us stop the normies," the boy explained.

"Holy mackerel! That is fangtastically frightening," Robecca muttered anxiously as steam poured out of her nostrils.

"There's no need to fog up the hall and frizz everyone's hair, we've finally found monsters who can help us," a soft voice called out.

"So I've heard," Robecca replied coldly as she watched Miss Flapper sashay down the hall, her long red locks bouncing against her back.

"I wonder where she's off to," Venus pondered aloud.

"To see Scariff Fred and Superintendent Petra," a voice chimed in.

"Jeez Louise! Where did you two come from?" Robecca yelped as she turned to see Jinafire and Skelita standing behind the group.

"Jinafire and I like to follow Senorita Flapper whenever we can. She's *muy interesante*. And with everything that's been happening we feel safer with her around," Skelita replied as she flicked her orange-and-black locks off her shoulder.

"You said she's on her way to see Scariff Fred and Superintendent Petra?" Cy repeated to the dragon and the *calaca*.

"That is *zhǔn què* or accurate as you say in Fanglish," Jinafire answered.

"And do you happen to know why she's meeting with them?" Venus inquired.

"To lobby on behalf of ASOME. To do everything in her power to make sure that we reach out to them in a timely fashion. For as the Fanghai proverb says, when there is only one chance, it must be nurtured, for without it there is nothing," Jinafire stated solemnly, before nodding her head and continuing on her way.

"*Adios, chicos*," Skelita added, and then proceeded after Jinafire.

"That proverb is not sitting well with me. ASOME is not an idea that I want to see nurtured. *Boo-la-la, quel désastre!*" Rochelle proclaimed as she shook her granite head side to side.

"We can't just sit by as Miss Flapper campaigns on behalf of ASOME," Venus remarked, and then began to grimace.

"Agreed. We need to do something to try and stop this wave of support before it's too late," Cy seconded.

And so that night over screamed corn and chicken à la vampire, Robecca, Rochelle, Venus, and Cy set about once again presenting their concerns to the puddle-prone Miss Sue Nami.

"There's more to ASOME than what Miss Flapper said. We've heard that they follow a monster hierarchy. They believe that certain creatures are superior to others," Venus said while shaking her head, clearly disturbed by what she was saying.

"How do you know this, non-adult entity?" Miss Sue Nami barked. "Have you personally dealt with ASOME?"

"Madame, we have heard things—" Rochelle started to reply, before being cut off by the ever-damp woman.

"Rumors? I don't have time for rumors. This whole town has been acting crazier than Clawdeen on a bad hair day, and all because of rumors. These normie stories have pushed Salem over the edge. Turned everyone's brains soggy with fear!" Monster High's acting headmistress groused.

"Miss Sue Nami, I don't mean any disrespect, but can you shake the water out of your ears—and I mean that literally and figuratively—because we need you to listen to us," Venus instructed.

"All clear and ready to hear," Miss Sue Nami answered, after pulling at both of her permanently pruned earlobes.

"Have we ever steered Monster High in the

139

wrong direction? Come on, just think of all we've done for this school. We've been like fertilizer to a plant, helping Monster High grow in all the right ways," Venus expounded.

"Do we have to be fertilizer in this analogy? What about being water or the sun? Not that there's anything wrong with fertilizer, it's just not the kind of thing you want to be compared to, well, not if you know what it's made out of anyway," Robecca muttered to herself as Rochelle motioned for the ghoul to bring her fertilizer soliloquy to a close.

"Careful, fertilizer is a very sensitive issue for plants. Insulting it is a bit like calling your kindhearted and helpful cousin unattractive. In other words, not very nice," Rochelle whispered.

"Um, Rochelle, it's nothing like that! Fertilizer is—oh, forget it—I don't have time to give you two a lesson on gardening!" Venus huffed, and then turned back to Miss Sue Nami. "What do you say? Will you help us?"

"Non-adult entities, you have done a lot for this school. I know that better than just about anyone. But on this one, I don't think you have enough information, or enough proof. And considering how bonkers everyone has been acting, I can't just push away the only chance of calming this lot down . . . not based on a rumor."

"But—" Venus tried to reply.

"But nothing. Bring me proof and I will support you ghouls. But without it, my hands are tied."

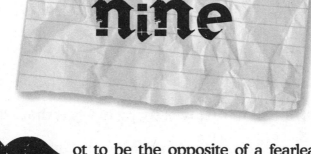

CHAPTER
nine

not to be the opposite of a fearleader—what would you call that? A Sour Sally? A Debbie Downer? A Frowning Freddie? Jeepers, I sure hope such terms don't offend all the Sallys, Debbies, and Freddies of the world," Robecca babbled while tucked into bed later that night.

"What are you saying, Robecca? Or is this more of a stream of consciousness discussion on names?" Venus asked.

"If that is in fact the case, I would like to add Tiresome Teddy and Gloomy Gilly to the list," Rochelle commented.

"I'm amazed we ever manage to finish a conversation. . . ." Venus trailed off as she rolled her eyes and smiled.

"Oh, forget it! All I was trying to say is that I don't know about this plan. I mean, even Penny looks a bit concerned by it," Robecca finally finished.

"That's Penny's natural expression, one of total disapproval. She's sort of like my great-aunt Fern and my grandma Hyacinth; no matter how much you water them, they're thirsty. If you open the blinds, they're getting too much sunlight; if you close them, not enough. Monsters like that are impossible to please," Venus clarified as she lay in bed dressed in bright green pajamas.

"While I agree with you, Venus, that Penny is impossible to please, I must also agree with Robecca. I too have concerns about your plan. And as any gargoyle will tell you, a poor plan is worse than no plan at all."

"Ghoulfriends! Get your heads out of the sand! We are in dire straits! We need to go big! We have no other option here!" Venus gestured animatedly.

"Our heads are most definitely not in the sand. And thankfully so, as sand can be very detrimental to mechanical monsters like Robecca."

"Rochelle!" Venus protested.

"However, you do seem to believe that this is our only course of action. And if there is one thing I have learned since my arrival at Monster High, it's that I trust my ghoulfriends," Rochelle continued.

"Wow, that was really impressive. You went from raising my pollens to melting my vines in less than thirty seconds," Venus admitted with a grin.

"But vines cannot melt," Rochelle pointed out.

"And back to the pollens."

"So it's settled," Robecca interjected uneasily. "Tomorrow during the assembly, we storm the stage and convince our classmates to rethink ASOME, or at the very least to investigate them further."

"Exactly," Venus replied.

"And if it doesn't work?" Robecca persisted.

"Then we run like crazy and hide from Miss Flapper. I'm pretty sure she's not going to be feeling very warm and fuzzy toward us after hearing what we have to say," Venus answered.

The next day Robecca, Rochelle, Venus, and Cy huddled in the back of the Catacombing classroom and muttered conspiratorially to one another as the teacher lectured. And though each was careful to whisper, the combination of four voices created a distracting hissing sound that quickly garnered the attention of other students and finally Mr. Mummy.

"Rochelle, I must say I am surprised at such behavior, talking during my safety lesson? How unbecoming a gargoyle!" Mr. Mummy said while shaking his gauze-covered head, both hands holding tight to his tweed and leather-trimmed vest.

"Monsieur Mummy, *je suis désolée*. I am very sorry. I am ashamed of my behavior. My gargoyle elders would be horrified!" Rochelle concurred, before dropping her head into her hands.

"It's all right this time, but let's not make it a habit," Mr. Mummy said, and then continued on with his speech.

"So we're going to storm the stage during the assembly?" Cy repeated back to Robecca, Rochelle, and Venus a short while later as the foursome dug for artifacts in the tunnels of the catacombs.

"I know it sounds crazier than flying across the country with a broken boiler, but it's the only idea we have," Robecca replied.

"But what makes you think anyone will even listen to us?" Cy asked.

"Cy makes a very good point," Rochelle inserted. "There is no reason for the students to listen to us; after all, we are not authority figures. We are not teachers or administrators. We are their peers, their equals."

"Yeah, the same peers that saved them from Miss Flapper's Whisper!" Venus blurted out as her vines tightened with tension.

"Venus, *s'il ghoul plaît*, there is no need to provoke your pollens."

"I'm sorry. I'm just frustrated at the idea that our voices may fall on deaf ears," Venus groaned.

"All we can do is remind our fellow students that we care for Monster High and that this is the only reason why we're asking for a proper investigation into ASOME," Cy said, before releasing a long sigh.

"*Regardez*, another old key," Rochelle said as she pulled a rusty object from the dirt.

"Maybe it's the key to wherever they're holding Headmistress Bloodgood and Wydowna . . . or maybe even where my dad is. . . ." Robecca prattled quietly to herself.

No matter how hard the ghoul tried, Robecca simply could not help but think of her father when in the Catacombs. It was, after all, the last place he was ever seen.

"We're going to find them, all three of them. And while I am not quite sure how we are going to do it, I am certain that this key will not be of any help," Rochelle responded, before tossing the key to Robecca with a wink.

The large Egyptian-themed Vampitheater was

chock-full of students and teachers when Superintendent Petra, Scariff Fred, and Miss Sue Nami entered. The threesome marched down the aisle confidently, clearly aware that every eye in the room was on them.

"Hello, non-adult entities," Miss Sue Nami announced loudly, after taking the stage with Scariff Fred and Superintendent Petra.

Seated directly in front of Miss Sue Nami, in the first row, were Cy, Robecca, Rochelle, and Venus. All of whom were twitching and fidgeting as they awaited the right moment to enact their plan.

"What is it about anticipation that rattles my rivets and dries up my hinges?" Robecca mumbled as Rochelle placed a reassuring hand on her leg.

"Scariff Fred and Superintendent Petra have

151

come here today to speak to you non-adult entities about a new program they are starting," Miss Sue Nami persisted.

"Step aside," Superintendent Petra grumbled as she grabbed the microphone. "We are here at Monster High to announce the student representative who, along with Miss Flapper, will personally reach out to ASOME to ask for help."

"You guys are the future, so it only seemed right that one of you should take part in saving it," Scariff Fred added while standing with his arms crossed over his belly.

From the middle of the Vampitheater came a scuffling sound.

"What are you doing? Sit down! You're wrinkling my shirt. And not just any old shirt, but a Moanatella Ghostier," Cleo growled loudly.

"Relax, gauze head," Toralei quipped. "I'm just being polite. I'm making my way to the aisle so that when they call my name I don't have to step on all these monsters to get there in a timely manner."

"What now?" Venus fretted. "Those two are always starting something."

"Perhaps we should seize this moment for our plan?" Rochelle suggested.

"I'd wait. If Toralei perceives us as stealing her thunder, we won't be able to quiet her down long enough to even speak," Cy pointed out.

"*C'est vrai*, it's true. She likes attention even more than Venus likes recycling," Rochelle acquiesced with a nod.

"Non-adult entity named Toralei," Miss Sue Nami yelled into the audience. "Sit down. You are not the student delegate who will be joining Miss Flapper."

"Ha! I knew it!" Cleo screamed happily as she started to push down the row of monsters, dragging Toralei behind her. "Royalty coming through, bow and move to the side!"

"You chose her? This is so wrong it should be illegal!" Toralei hissed.

"Take a seat, Cleo!" Miss Sue Nami cautioned.

As the two dueling divas returned to their chairs, Superintendent Petra pulled an envelope from her pocket and began to open it, all the while remaining as expressionless as ever.

"Ready, ghouls and guy?" Venus said to the others as she popped out of her chair and started for the stage with Rochelle and Cy behind her.

"I don't know," Robecca started to answer, before noting her friends' hasty departures. "I guess that was a rhetorical question," she muttered to herself as she moved quickly to catch up with the trio.

"What are you doing? You were not chosen either!" Miss Sue Nami yelled. "What is wrong with you non-adult entities today?"

"Return to your seats, now! I do not take kindly to acts of insubordination," Superintendent Petra fired at the foursome.

"Unfortunately, madame, we must disobey your request at this time. We are all very sorry to do so, but the circumstances require it," Rochelle replied politely as Venus snatched the microphone.

"Put down the microphone," Scariff Fred added, oozing exasperation.

"Sorry, Scariff Fred, but I can't do that. We can't do that. We care too much about this school to just stand by while we all make the biggest mistake of our lives," Venus explained.

"Or unlives, as the case may be," Rochelle interjected on behalf of the ghosts and other dead creatures in the audience.

"There is more to ASOME than what we've been told—" Venus tried to continue, before being drowned out.

"I have had just about enough of this behavior!" Superintendent Petra hollered.

"Yes, I agree! Remove them from the stage this instance!" Miss Flapper called out from the audience.

"Hold on, Miss Flapper," a man's voice boomed through the Vampitheater, bouncing off the purple walls.

As the audience turned to see who it was,

Venus answered their question.

"Dracula!" the plant ghoul uttered into the microphone.

"Dad? What are you doing here?" Draculaura asked loudly from her seat in the audience.

"Trying to stop the worst thing that could ever happen to the monster community. And I'm not here alone," Dracula said as Mrs. Gorgon, Mr. Stein, Mr. and Mrs. Wolf, Mrs. Yelps, and Mr. De Nile walked into the Vampitheater after him.

CHAPTER
ten

"We are here today to reveal a secret. A secret we have guarded for many decades," Dracula stated, after taking to the stage with Mrs. Gorgon, Mr. and Mrs. Wolf, Mrs. Yelps, Mr. Stein, and Mr. De Nile.

"Scariff Fred? Are you just going to allow students and now parents to hijack your assembly? This is hardly appropriate behavior!" Miss Flapper chastised the man from her seat.

"While I understand your frustration, Miss

Flapper, these parents are well-respected members of the community. So I feel it's only right that we at least hear them out."

"Thank you, Scariff," Dracula said as Venus motioned for Cy, Robecca, and Rochelle to follow her back to their seats in the front row. "ASOME stands for the Ancient Society of Monster Elite. It is an organization that believes in a hierarchy of monsters. That is to say that vampires, mummies, and aristocratic ghosts make up the ruling class, which governs over all other creatures."

The Vampitheater was not only quiet but still, as though every monster had been momentarily paralyzed by the information.

"I know this to be true because I used to be a member of ASOME back in the Old World. But I myself began to see that all monsters are created

160

equal, and was increasingly bothered by the group's failure to see this. And so I and Ramses de Nile left ASOME. We then came to the Boo World, where we met up with other monsters who shared our beliefs. Together we have worked tirelessly to keep ASOME out of the Boo World and out of Salem. It's why we opened Monster High," Dracula continued. "And when I say we, I mean all those that stand before you today. We are the Society of United Monsters."

"What?" Deuce remarked. "It's like I don't even know my own mom! She's a member of a secret group?"

"Tell me about it!" Frankie seconded. "What's next? My last name's not really Stein!"

"Not to worry, our last name is Stein," Mr. Stein reassured his daughter as Dracula continued speaking.

"One of our members is not with us today, but as

his daughter sits in the audience, I would very much like to acknowledge him. Hexiciah Steam."

"Whaaaaaa—?" Robecca muttered as her eyes bulged and steam flew from her ears at a speed that Rochelle and Venus had never seen before.

"We also owe a great debt to Headmistress Bloodgood, who helped us start Monster High," Mr. Wolf added. "And after years of working together, I feel confident stating that she would not support reaching out to ASOME, regardless of whom we were up against."

"The list we found in the attic. It was the members of the Society of United Monsters," Venus squealed to Rochelle.

"Yes, but Ramses de Nile was not on the list," Rochelle said as she rubbed her chin.

"It must have been a mistake," Venus responded as Miss Flapper jumped out of her seat and glided up to the stage.

"Excuse me, excuse me. But I simply must say something. I can no longer hold my tongue," Miss Flapper said in her usual soft manner.

"Of course," Dracula responded politely, and then motioned for her to take the microphone.

"While this new information about ASOME momentarily left me puzzled, it has not changed my mind. Wouldn't you rather deal with a ruling class of educated monsters that maintains an ordered society than live like prisoners under normie rule? I know I would."

The Vampitheater instantly erupted in shrieks and cries as the ghouls and boys of Monster High began debating the issue. Rochelle, Cy, and Venus looked around them as their peers' voices grew louder and louder. Meanwhile, shell-shocked

Robecca stood up and slowly walked to the stage.

"This isn't the bee's knees. This is the whole bee's body! My dad was a part of your group? He helped start Monster High?" Robecca babbled to Dracula, Mr. and Mrs. Wolf, Mr. De Nile, Mrs. Yelps, Mr. Stein, and Mrs. Gorgon.

"Your father was a normie who understood monsters. He was a great man, and we all hope to see him again one day," Dracula responded.

"Do you have any clue where he might be? What might have happened to him?"

"Unfortunately, young lady, we do not have any information as to your father's current whereabouts," Mr. De Nile replied coldly.

"But that doesn't mean we won't see him again," Mrs. Gorgon said kindly, adjusting her large black sunglasses.

"Do you know what he was doing when he disappeared in the catacombs?" Robecca asked as she felt a heavy hand land on her shoulder.

"*Chérie*, are you okay?" Rochelle asked as she, Venus, and Cy surrounded their blue-haired friend.

"Yes, I am," Robecca replied with a smile. "I'm more than okay—I'm the cat's pajamas! Turns out, my dad is even more amazing than I thought!"

"That he is," Dracula responded. "And to answer your question, he was supposed to meet Ramses in the catacombs, but he never showed up."

"At first I was very offended. Standing up royalty is hardly appropriate. But then I realized something must be very wrong. And indeed it was," Ramses de Nile responded.

"Mr. De Nile, do you mind if I ask you a question?" Venus interjected.

"Of course not, I know how interested ghouls are in the monarchy," Ramses de Nile responded.

"Maybe other ghouls, but not me," Venus explained, much to the mummy's displeasure. "My question is about your stance on ASOME. You're against it, right?"

"What a thing to ask! I'm a member of the Society of United Monsters!" Ramses de Nile huffed.

"Sorry, I didn't mean to offend you. It's just that Cleo mentioned something about you being in support of ASOME," Venus clarified.

"My daughter must have had gauze in her ears. I have only ever told her that I am against ASOME. She probably just got confused, as her aunt Neferia, who is visiting from the Old World, is a bit partial to the antiquated manner in which ASOME approaches life."

"Well, thanks for clearing that up," Venus said with a tense smile.

By the time the final bell sounded, Monster High had descended into a mass of arguments over which risk to take—ASOME or the normies.

"ASOME goes against everything that Monster High was founded upon," Draculaura stated forcefully to a messily clad mummy in the hall.

"Yeah, but I don't want to live in Salem if the town is a jail! I would rather live by the laws of mummies, vampires, and aristocratic ghosts!" the boy cried.

"Easy for you to say. You're a mummy," Lagoona chimed in as she walked up to Draculaura and the boy.

"What do you suggest we do, then?" he muttered.

"That's the hard part, mate. I don't know. I just know that ASOME will destroy everything I believe in," Lagoona replied.

"It seems nothing is easy. We may have slowed the support for ASOME, but now everyone's arguing," Robecca said to Rochelle and Venus as they made their way to the dormitory.

"Monster High divided as school decides whose rule they would prefer to live under," Spectra announced as she floated past the trio in the corridor. "For the latest news, check out my blog!"

"Our classmates might be arguing, but that's a whole lot better than everyone supporting ASOME," Venus said to Rochelle and Robecca as they mounted the creaky pink rot-iron stairs to the dormitory.

"I doubt she sees it that way," Robecca mumbled to her ghoulfriends as she spotted Miss Flapper at the top of the staircase.

"Is madame crying?" Rochelle asked the others as Miss Flapper looked at the trio and then turned around and headed back down the dormitory hall.

"What was that about?" Venus wondered as she bounded up the staircase after the graceful European dragon.

Leaning against the wall and quietly sniffling, Miss Flapper did not even look up when Robecca, Rochelle, and Venus approached.

"Madame Flapper, we are most sorry to see that you are so upset. Is everything all right?" Rochelle asked while offering the woman a pale pink Scaremès scarf.

"Is everything all right? No! Everything is not all right!" Miss Flapper answered, and then took the scarf and dabbed her tears. "I just heard from Scariff Fred and Superintendent Petra that Cleo and Toralei were abducted by normies while walking home from school this afternoon."

CHAPTER
eleven

*J*e ne comprends pas. I don't understand. I thought the scariff's deputies were escorting students between school and their homes," Rochelle questioned Miss Flapper.

"Apparently Cleo and Toralei wandered off and then . . ." Miss Flapper said, before gasping and shaking her head.

"And then what?" Venus persisted.

"And then they were grabbed by normies," Miss Flapper muttered.

"Who told you this? Is there someone who can confirm that Cleo and Toralei were abducted by *normies*?" Venus pushed back.

"Cleo's Aunt Neferia. She was in town doing some shopping when she saw three menacing normies grab the ghouls. She tried to stop them, but she was too far away," Miss Flapper explained. "I feel terrible. If only Scariff Fred had listened to me and contacted ASOME earlier today. Then maybe this wouldn't have happened."

"Somehow I doubt that," Venus replied flatly.

"The only silver lining in any of this is that now Ramses de Nile is supporting reaching out to ASOME. He has seen the light. He realizes that without their help, he might never see his daughter again," Miss Flapper said dramatically. "Now if you'll excuse me, I'm off to see Scariff Fred. I must talk some sense into the man. There isn't much time left."

Seated on the floor of their dorm room with their pets, the trio processed the information that Miss Flapper had presented to them.

"Cleo's Aunt Neferia saw them being abducted?" Venus repeated back to the others.

"From what I remember of Neferia de Nile from the Crier's Club, she wears pretty thick glasses. So maybe she thought the abductors were normies, but they were actually just other monsters," Robecca hypothesized.

"Or maybe she's working with ASOME. Ramses said that his sister was partial to some of ASOME's ideas," Venus remembered.

"*Boo-la-la*! Just when we stopped the school from seeing ASOME as the only answer, this happens," Rochelle lamented.

"I doubt it's an accident. Think about it: Fear of more abductions will drive monsters back to supporting ASOME," Venus replied.

"If only the normie mayor could come to Salem and reassure everyone," Robecca blathered. "But of course with our borders closed, that's pretty much impossible."

"Is it? There has to be some way for us to at least get a video of him saying that they aren't planning on walling us in," Venus said as she bit her lip and pondered the situation.

"I feel it is my duty to point out that while the normies are not dangerous, they are not necessarily friendly either," Rochelle explained.

"I know that the normies aren't crazy about us monsters, but I bet if we told the mayor our situation he would make a video. If only just to avoid any

174

future complications," Venus supposed.

"So that just leaves the border," Robecca offered, before breaking into a smirk. "We could dig a tunnel!"

"*C'est ridicule.* That is ridiculous!" Rochelle chimed in as Robecca started to giggle.

"What if we dress up like trolls? No one cares where they go."

"*Boo-la-la*, Robecca. That is even more absurd!"

"She's joking, Rochelle," Venus said as she shook her head.

"Wait, I have an idea, a serious one!" Robecca yelped. "What if I jetted us across?"

"Surprisingly, that might actually work," Venus piped up with excitement.

"*C'est vrai.* It's true that could work. But it is also possible that one of the scariff's deputies could try and bring Robecca down with a bow and arrow."

"I would like to officially withdraw my suggestion now," Robecca responded.

"What was your first idea again, Robecca?" Rochelle asked while rubbing her chin.

"Digging a tunnel? I think that would take a really long time. Plus, without the help of contractors, our tunnel could collapse, and it doesn't take a gargoyle to know how dangerous that would be," Robecca replied.

"*Jamais!* Never would I allow *us* to build a tunnel! Well, at least not without the proper plans and professionals on hand," Rochelle huffed. "However, I think there might already be a tunnel in place that we could use."

"What are you talking about? And how come you never mentioned this before?" Venus blustered.

"I am not certain that I am correct. But as I was

176

thinking about Robecca's father—" Rochelle began to explain.

"My father?"

"Yes, about how he was last seen in the catacombs. And from there I started thinking about how the catacombs predate both Salem and Monster High, and that's when it occurred to me, there might be a tunnel that leads into the normie town," Rochelle finished.

"How can we find out for sure?" Venus asked.

"When it comes to the catacombs, no one knows more than Monsieur Mummy."

"Don't let your son or daughter be next! Support ASOME today!" Ramses de Nile proclaimed while marching back and forth with Toralei's guardian, Tab Bee, in front of Monster High's main entrance.

"I need ASOME! You need ASOME! We all need ASOME!" Tab Bee chanted.

"Wow," Venus remarked to Robecca and Rochelle. "A two-person picket line."

"And now here comes their fearleader," Rochelle mumbled as she watched Miss Flapper gracefully walk out the front door and up to the two men.

"Bravo! We must show everyone that without ASOME, we have no chance for a future," Miss Flapper commended the two men.

"And now for the fearleader's fearleaders," Robecca added as Jinafire and Skelita trailed after Miss Flapper.

"Come on, ghouls, let's head to the Creepateria. They're about to stop serving breakfast," Venus said, before turning and walking into Monster High's main hall.

A few hours later, as the trio approached the gilded elevator to the catacombs, Rochelle heard a familiar voice. One that used to send chills of excitement up her cold granite spine.

"Rochelle! Hey!" Deuce's voice carried down the hall.

"Ah, Deuce, *chérie*, how are you holding up?" Rochelle offered kindly as the sunglasses-clad boy approached.

"I really miss Cleo. But you know what's crazy? I've gotten so used to Toralei that I even miss her a little too," Deuce replied.

"As you know, Cleo and I didn't always see eye to eye, while Toralei and I barely spoke the same language," Venus stated candidly. "But all the same, I was really sorry to hear what happened to them."

"Me too. Luckily, I'm pretty confident that they will be returned shortly," Deuce explained. "Dealing with Toralei and Cleo is not easy. Actually, sometimes it can be downright tortuous. Whoever took them will figure that out soon enough."

"And what about ASOME? Do you think we should reach out to them?" Robecca questioned Deuce.

"I just don't know. My mom says they will destroy us, but Mr. De Nile says that they are the only ones who can help bring Cleo back."

"What time is it?" Robecca suddenly blurted out. "Where's Penny?"

"For once Robecca's outburst about the time is

actually spot on. It is, in fact, time we head down for Catacombing, as we have something to discuss with Monsieur Mummy before class," said Rochelle.

"But what about Penny? Did I leave her in the buffet line in the Creepateria again? You know how she dislikes buffets. Oh dear, she's probably pelting the cook with food by now!" Robecca squeaked as her face contorted with concern.

"Not to worry, I've got Penny," Cy interjected as he walked up behind the group, the grumpy penguin in his arms.

"Ah! Thank you! And look, Penny isn't scowling as much as usual! Why, that's almost like a smile for her!" Robecca proclaimed.

After riding down in the ornate gold elevator, the group made their way into the classroom where Mr. Mummy unpacked his valise.

Deuce quickly found himself in deep conversation with Hoodude, who was petrified that Frankie might be the next normie target. Cy, Robecca, and Venus huddled in the corner and watched as Rochelle approached their teacher.

"Monsieur Mummy, might I have a word with you before class starts?" Rochelle inquired of her dapperly dressed teacher.

"Is this about your proposal to add a first aid room down here? Because I have not been able to speak with Miss Sue Nami yet. As you know, things at Monster High haven't exactly been going smoothly," Mr. Mummy said, pursing his lips.

"While I am still very much in support of a first aid room being added to the catacombs, I am actually here on other business today. It's about the tunnels. Do you know if there is one that extends beneath the normie town?"

"Why are you asking me this, Rochelle?" Mr. Mummy answered with widening eyes.

"The Gargoyle Code of Ethics, paragraph 56.8, states that students should not fib to teachers, and so with that in mind, I shall be truthful with you."

"Go on," Mr. Mummy said as he motioned for an approaching student to back away.

"Robecca, Venus, and I do not believe that the normies are a threat to us. We believe that ASOME is behind all of this. That they have fabricated the normie ruse so that we freely place ourselves under their rule."

"Excuse me?" Mr. Mummy uttered in shock.

"They have long been trying to gain a foothold in the Boo World, and now they are about to get one. And from here, there will be little to stop them from growing their influence."

"You know, very few people give gargoyles credit for having imagination. But clearly that is not the case, as you are quite the tall-tale teller."

"Monsieur Mummy, I assure you, I am not."

"I am not a fan of ASOME. I do not adhere to this idea that a select group of creatures should have all the power. But I do not for a second believe that they crafted this normie story. In case you've forgotten, a parent has spoken to the normie mayor, seen plans for the wall, even a Fearbook with circled faces."

"Then this anonymous parent must be in on it. That is the only viable explanation," Rochelle responded.

"And the yarn continues. . . ." Mr. Mummy said with a sigh while shaking his head back and forth.

Across the room, Venus, Robecca, and Cy watched the encounter closely.

184

"I may not be able to read lips, but I can read body language. Rochelle is bombing this, as in going down in flames," Venus muttered to the others.

"Jeepers, I think you're right. Mr. Mummy just rolled his eyes at her last comment," Robecca remarked as small steam puffs exited her ears.

"Is it too late to abort the mission?" Cy asked.

"I think we're in search-and-rescue mode now. As in search for a way out and attempt to rescue our plan," Venus replied, and then strutted across the room and threw her arm around Rochelle.

"Venus," Mr. Mummy said with palpable aggravation. "Please don't tell me that you too believe this nonsense story about ASOME making up the normie threat."

"What? No way! That is pure fiction! I tell you, Mr. Mummy, Rochelle has become a bit paranoid with all that's been going on."

"*Pardonnez-moi*—?" Rochelle squawked as Venus's hand landed atop her stone lips to shush her.

"As I was saying, Rochelle has kind of lost her grasp on what's been happening. She's even been talking about crawling through one of the catacombs' tunnels so she can visit the normie town," Venus continued.

Mr. Mummy shook his head, visibly disturbed by the news.

"Which of course doesn't even exist, right?" Venus prodded her teacher.

"Well, it exists, but it's long been boarded up," Mr. Mummy answered reticently.

"And where is it exactly?" Venus continued.

"Why do you ask?" Mr. Mummy persisted suspiciously.

"In case this crazy little gargoyle sneaks off, at least I will know where to look for her," Venus explained with a stiff smile.

"Class is about to begin," Mr. Mummy remarked as he glanced at his watch.

"Please, you know how much my ghoulfriends mean to me. Help me keep this one safe," Venus pleaded as she motioned toward Rochelle.

"Very well. The southeast corner, just past the portrait of anthropologist Jane Ghoulall," Mr. Mummy answered as he picked up his roll call sheet.

"Thank you, Mr. Mummy," Venus said as she pulled Rochelle away, her green hand still firmly placed across the granite ghoul's mouth.

"Mission accomplished, courtesy of yours truly," Venus said triumphantly as they walked up to Cy and Robecca.

"I only hope that I do not contract some kind of bacterial infection from having your hand atop my mouth. I couldn't help but notice that your hand did not smell of soap, which is most definitely not a good sign," Rochelle explained as she applied anti-bacterial lip gloss, a Scarisian specialty.

"Tonight we're heading into a foreign land, or at least we're trying to," Venus proclaimed to her visibly nervous friends, ignoring Rochelle's germaphobia. "It won't be easy, but if it works, we'll save Salem and Monster High."

"And if it doesn't work?" Rochelle inquired.

"Then we're back to square one? Or we're in a normie prison? It could go either way," Venus replied matter-of-factly.

188

As the clock's hands hovered over the twelve, Robecca, Rochelle, Cy, and Venus stepped onto the ornate golden elevator to the catacombs.

"*Boo la la*! Venturing into the catacombs after midnight is definitely a *non-non*," Rochelle wondered aloud as she tapped her claws against her cheek.

"We're fighting a war, in case you haven't noticed," Venus shot back. "And in war, like in love, there are no rules."

"*S'il ghoul plaît*, Venus! Must you say such things to me? You know how much rules mean to me."

"We're here," Cy said as the elevator doors opened into the catacombs.

First out of the elevator, the boy opened the heart-shaped rot-iron gate, above which hung a hand-carved sign: WELCOME TO THE NORTHERN TUNNELS OF THE CATACOMBS, WHERE HIDDEN FROM LIGHT, IN THE

DARK OF NIGHT, YOU JUST MIGHT FIND A MONSTER'S TRUEST FRIGHT.

"Mr. Mummy said it was in the southeast corner, just past the portrait of anthropologist Jane Ghoulall," Venus informed the others.

Dimly lit rot-iron sconces, carvings of skulls, and portraits of historically relevant figures adorned the gray stone walls. Everyone from Thomas Deadison to Franklin Delano Growlsevelt seemed to be watching them as the group crept along the drafty corridor.

"It's kind of spooky down here," Robecca whispered.

"Spooky? I do not agree. Unless of course you are referring to the possibility of bumping into something and stubbing your toe or banging your shin?" Rochelle asked.

"Bumping into something? How about someone?

190

Wouldn't it be fangtastic to happen upon my father down here?" Robecca whispered excitedly.

"The Gargoyle Code of Ethics paragraph 76.2 states that managing a friend's expectations is key to maintaining a lifelong friendship. Therefore, I must tell you that it is highly unlikely that we will just run into your father down here."

"Jane Ghoulall!" Cy called out excitedly, and then turned the corner and gasped.

"Talk about a flea's tease! How are we ever going to get through that?" Robecca asked after she walked around the corner.

A mess of nails, wood, and even a thick metal chain covered the entrance of the tunnel to the normie town. It was, in short, impenetrable.

CHAPTER twelve

"What time is it?" Robecca cried while splayed out beneath a small pile of debris, her copper eyelids fighting to stay open after hours of hard work trying to break through the barrier.

"Robecca! Stop asking what time it is and help us!" Venus snapped.

"It's six fifteen AM," Cy whispered to Robecca after checking that Venus wasn't listening.

"My fingers have so many splinters in them, they look like cacti. Not to mention I think I pulled a root," Venus lamented.

"We're almost through, *chéries*," Rochelle encouraged the others as she stifled a yawn.

"Almost through is not through," Venus grumbled as she blew strands of pink hair off her forehead.

"Plants are *très grognons*, or grouchy as you say in Fanglish, when they don't get enough sleep," Rochelle muttered to Cy. "*Quel dommage*. What a shame, for us that is. . . ."

"I heard that," Venus grunted as she yanked at a piece of wood, which triggered a strange creaking noise.

"*Errr . . . err . . .*"

"What is that?" Cy asked.

"An animal? You know how normies love to

194

have exotic pets. Maybe one got loose and wound up down here!" Robecca rambled.

"That seems highly unlikely, although it's true that normies like to have odd pets. I once read an article about a man who kept a tiger in his one-bedroom apartment in Boo York," Rochelle stated as Venus pulled at another piece of wood in the wall.

"It's not an animal; it's the wood," Venus explained, seconds before the wall started to crumble, piece by piece.

"Bravo! Venus! Bravo!" Rochelle cried excitedly.

"Good golly, Miss Molly, you sure are strong," Robecca remarked.

"What can I tell you? My vines are tougher than they look," Venus responded proudly.

"Yikes! It's pretty dark in there," Robecca said as she followed Cy into the near pitch-black tunnel.

"Luckily for you, you are traveling with a gargoyle. And as you know, gargoyles come prepared," Rochelle said as she pulled out a flashlight.

"And we're sure this is the right tunnel? This is the one that leads to the normie town?" Cy asked the others.

"That's what Mr. Mummy said. . . ." Venus trailed off as she looked anxiously around the space. "I hope he knows what he's talking about."

The foursome walked through the murky and musty-smelling corridor for what felt like hours. Though it was, in fact, only forty-seven minutes.

"Ouch!" Venus screeched as she bumped into one of the many discarded chairs and sconces littered across the floor of the tunnel.

"*Regardez*! I see something! Slivers of light up above!" Rochelle called out.

"It's a manhole," Cy assessed as the foursome stood looking up at the splinters of light.

"A what?" Robecca asked.

"You know, those metal things in the streets that lead to sewers and other stuff below cities. In this case, a catacombs tunnel," Cy replied.

"How are we going to do this? Are we all just walking into normieville? Or should only one of us go?" Venus asked the others.

"One monster might sneak through town unnoticed, but four? I doubt it. But it must be noted that it's far more dangerous for whoever goes alone. For even though the normies are not actually threatening to wall us in, they aren't used to us. The sight of a monster popping up in town might frighten some of them," Rochelle hypothesized.

"I'll go," Cy stated.

"Why?" Venus asked. "And don't say because you're a boy. Because ghouls are just as strong as boys."

"It has nothing to do with the fact that I am a boy. You guys are a trio, I don't think you could function without one another."

"That is so sweet!" Robecca gushed as she started to steam up.

"And highly codependent," Rochelle interjected.

"Please know, Cy, we need you too," Robecca finished.

"Thanks."

"It's almost seven thirty AM. If you are going to do this, you should go now, before the streets become crowded," Rochelle advised.

"You need to find the mayor's office," Venus said,

and then paused. "Once there, figure out a way inside so that you can convince him to make a video stating that the normies have no intention of walling us in," Venus instructed.

"I have a bad feeling about this! What if the mayor is afraid of monsters and throws Cy in jail? Then we really will have to reach out to ASOME for help!" Robecca squealed.

"It is true that the normie/monster relationship has a long and difficult history. There have been pockets of trouble as well as friendship over the years," Rochelle responded.

"Well, here's to hoping we're in a pocket of friendship," Cy said unsurely as he pulled up one of the abandoned chairs from the tunnel and climbed atop it.

Light flooded into the damp space as Cy pushed

the manhole to the side
and then slowly pulled
himself to the street.

"*Bonne chance*! Good luck!" Rochelle wished the boy.

"Stay safe!" Robecca called out as Cy pushed the manhole back in place and disappeared into normieville.

"My vines are so tense I think they might snap in half," Venus commented as the trio sat in the faint light of the tunnel.

"Jeez Louise! How long has he been gone? An hour? Two? He's probably in normie jail by now!"

"Becs, Cy's been gone eight minutes," Venus replied. "And please stop talking about jail. It's hardly helping the mood."

"Then what should we talk about? The mayor?

What do we know about him? Is he nice? Is he young? Is he old? Does he like karaoke? Monsters with one eye?" Robecca babbled.

"We don't know anything about him except that he is *not* threatening to wall us in," said Rochelle.

"But what if we're wrong? What if everything Miss Flapper said is true? They'll kidnap Cy just like they did Wydowna and Headmistress Bloodgood!" Robecca squawked.

"Venus, *s'il ghoul plaît*, help me hold Robecca's hands. Our ghoulfriend needs to calm down."

Minutes passed like hours and hours passed like days as Robecca, Rochelle, and Venus waited for Cy to return to the tunnel. He had been gone two hours and thirteen minutes, which was exactly thirteen minutes longer than either Venus or Rochelle had anticipated.

"There's no way the normies are really planning to wall us in, right?" Robecca questioned her friends.

"For the last time, no," Venus replied, albeit with a slightly shaky voice.

"Are you sure about that? Because you don't sound that sure."

"Robecca, Venus is as sure as I am, which I place at approximately seventy-eight percent."

"What? Why only seventy-eight percent?!" Robecca yelped.

"I came into this tunnel at a hundred percent, but there is something about sitting in the dark that has eroded my ability to think clearly," Rochelle confessed.

"I know! It's like some kind of terrible torture. It's worse than watching an aluminum can get thrown into the trash," Venus seconded.

"What's that?" Robecca yelped. "Is that a siren? An ambulance? The police? The MIA, the Monster Intelligence Agency?"

"I don't hear anything. So either you're imagining something or I'm going deaf," Venus replied.

"Both of you stop talking! I have come to believe that conversing of any kind is highly detrimental to our mental health," Rochelle instructed the others as the sound of the manhole scratching against the pavement echoed through the tunnel.

"Cy's back!" Robecca said with relief, before gasping. "Unless of course he caved under normie questioning and it's actually the police coming to arrest us for trespassing!"

203

"Trespassing! An arrest record! Those are not terms gargoyles want to hear," Rochelle cried, before a bright light flooded the tunnel, suddenly blinding the trio. The intense burst of sunlight left the ghouls seeing spots of color even after Cy closed the manhole cover behind him.

"These dots of light I'm seeing are beautiful, but not as beautiful as seeing Cy again!" Robecca exclaimed.

"Sorry, ghouls, I should have warned you to close your eyes," Cy apologized.

"We're just glad to see you," said Venus as the foursome started on their way back through the tunnel toward Monster High. "Now tell us what happened!"

"Mayor Mazin is a really nice guy, and smart too," Cy reflected.

"Is that why you spent so much time with him?" Venus persisted.

"I spent most of the time trying to find the mayor's office. You have to remember that walking around a normie town with a big eye in the middle of your forehead without being noticed is *not* easy. Even with the hood of my sweatshirt pulled down over half my face I couldn't ask for directions, so I just had to keep wandering until I found the office."

"And what happened when you found the office? You simply walked in and said, '*Boo-jour*, I am a monster and I must talk to the mayor'?" Rochelle inquired.

"Hardly," Cy replied with a chuckle. "The mayor's secretary looked about as friendly as Superintendent Petra after spending time with Miss Sue Nami."

"So how did you get to the mayor?" Robecca chimed in.

205

"I climbed up a tree in front of the building and then I jumped from there to the roof—"

"Jeepers! Who knew Cy was a spider ghoul?" Robecca remarked excitedly.

"Then I almost crashed to the ground as I attempted to lower myself onto the mayor's balcony from the roof. But eventually I climbed through the window and introduced myself," Cy continued.

"How did he respond? A monster climbing through his window unannounced? That could be pretty jarring," Venus supposed.

"Surprisingly well. It turns out his parents once sent him to a monster and normie camp in upstate Boo York, so he's more comfortable around creatures than the average normie."

"What are they like? I've never been around any normies," Robecca admitted.

"They seemed fine, except, well . . ."

"What?" Robecca inquired.

"They're really boring dressers. I've never seen so much khaki and beige in my life. It's like they're afraid of color or something."

"While I am amused by their fashion limitations, I must ask you, did you get the video?" Rochelle cut to the chase.

"Yes, I did," Cy replied confidently, clearly proud of what he had accomplished.

"YEAH!!" Robecca squealed.

"*Merci boo-coup!*"

"Okay, that does it, we're no longer a trio. We are now officially a quartet," Venus said while patting Cy on the arm.

"Thanks, ghouls!" Cy replied, his face locked in a permanent smile.

CHAPTER
thirteen

ake up, you lot!" Ms. Kindergrubber hollered at Cy, Venus, Rochelle, and Robecca as each of them dozed off during Home Ick. They had arrived to campus so late that they didn't even have time to change, let alone sleep.

"It's bad enough I have to deal with these two," Ms. Kindergrubber continued as she flung open the pantry doors where Rose and Blanche Van Sangre were sleeping among the dried goods, covered in crumbs.

"Vhat time is it?" Rose muttered as her eyes creaked open.

"Time zo go back zo sleep," Blanche replied as she popped a cookie into her mouth. "I think ve might have found the perfect place zo nap."

"I know. Eating vhile ve sleep—this is the life," Rose trailed off, and then quickly started snoring.

Ms. Kindergrubber slammed the cupboard shut and shook her head at Venus, Cy, Robecca, and Rochelle.

"*Boo-la-la! Je suis désolée*, madame! We had very little sleep last night. Hence why we were nodding off atop our cutting boards," Rochelle explained as Ms. Kindergrubber mumbled to herself and then walked away.

210

"Hey, ghouls," Frankie called over to Robecca, Rochelle, and Venus. "I don't know if you heard, but I'm canceling today's Frightingale meeting because of the Claws & Gauze Summit."

"The what?" Venus questioned Frankie.

"The Claws & Gauze Summit to honor Toralei and Cleo," Frankie explained. "Spectra announced it this morning on her blog. Apparently Cleo's dad and Toralei's guardian set it up with Miss Flapper. I think Scariff Fred and Superintendent Petra are coming as well to show their respect for the missing ghouls."

"My dad says it's just another ruse by Miss Flapper to garner support for ASOME, which is probably true. But I'm attending anyway. I might not be Toralei's biggest fan, but I want them both home just as much as the rest of you," Draculaura added.

"Are you ghouls going to attend?" Frankie asked.

"We wouldn't miss it for the world," Venus replied.

"We wouldn't?" Robecca wondered aloud, before catching Rochelle's eye. "I mean, we wouldn't. That is to say, we'll be there."

The Claws & Gauze Summit was held in the Study Howl classroom, which had been transformed into a shrine to Toralei and Cleo, their pictures covering every available inch of wall space.

"It really is such a shame that neither of them are here to appreciate this *fangtastique* ode to them. I am quite certain that they would be thrilled. After all, you know how much they like to look at

themselves," Rochelle said while surveying the surroundings.

"Isn't that the truth?" Frankie said with a laugh. "Cleo once told me that the best birthday gift she ever received was a mirror."

"Toralei once asked me to sign a petition to name her Monster High's Greatest . . . well, everything," Draculaura added with a smile. "You ghouls have to admit she's a great source of comedy."

"They both are, mate. Just last week they offered to give me swimming lessons. Apparently, the two of them think they can swim better than a sea creature!" Lagoona remembered as she, Frankie, and Draculaura headed across the room to find seats.

"Jeepers, does anyone else feel bad that we're having a Claws & Gauze Summit instead of a Headless & Webbed & Claws & Gauze Summit? After all, Cleo and Toralei aren't the only ones missing," Robecca noted to Cy, Venus, and Rochelle.

"You really do have the biggest heart," Cy responded to Robecca. "I'm surprised it can even fit in there."

"Technically speaking, I do not believe Robecca has an actual heart but a . . ." Rochelle trailed off after Venus nudged her.

"Thanks, Cy," Robecca responded bashfully. "I think your heart is even bigger than your eye. . . . Wait, that sounded weird, didn't it? I meant it as a compliment!"

"I know, I know," Cy said with a laugh. "You never need to worry with me. I think it's pretty clear we understand each other."

"Look, there's Miss Flapper with Ramses de Nile and Tab Bee. I don't know about you guys, but I am super pumped to play the video," Venus said while fidgeting with her vines.

"We're all set on that front," Cy said with a satisfied smile.

The Claws & Gauze Summit kicked off with Ramses de Nile and Tab Bee speaking about their deep-seated fear that Cleo and Toralei would never be returned to Salem, since the monsters lack the necessary power to pressure the normies. Then, as if following a script, Miss Flapper took the microphone and once again spoke of ASOME.

"Life doesn't always afford us perfect situations

or easy decisions. Sometimes we need to make hard calls. Tough calls. Choices that will protect the future. ASOME is our only chance. Time is running out. Please tell Scariff Fred that you support reaching out to ASOME. Otherwise, there's sure to be more abductions of beautiful young ghouls just like these two," Miss Flapper said as she pushed a button, prompting a screen to pop up. "Here is a montage of a few of our favorite memories of Cleo and Toralei."

However, instead of Cleo and Toralei, a friendly-looking normie with a thick mustache, dressed in a suit and tie, appeared on screen.

"Who's that normie?" Superintendent Petra screeched.

"Hello, my name is Darren Mazin, and I am the mayor of

216

the town next to Salem," the man said as though he were answering Superintendent Petra's question. "A young man came to see me today about a rumor that we were planning to build a wall to separate us normies from you monsters. Well, I am here today to tell you that nothing could be farther from the truth. As a matter of fact, at the last town council meeting we voted to extend an invite to our monster neighbors for our Fall Festival."

"I don't understand!" Superintendent Petra screamed. Her eyes darted around the Study Howl until she spotted Ramses de Nile.

"You told us that you met with the normie mayor. That you saw the plans for the wall?" Scariff Fred said as he approached the now stressed-looking mummy.

"I am royalty! A scaraoh! I am only protecting

217

my history, my legacy!" Ramses de Nile hollered in response.

"But you're a member of the Society of United Monsters?" Robecca screamed at she stood up in the crowd.

"I was, but then my sister Neferia helped me realize that ASOME is right. Traditions must be continued! Family legacies must thrive!"

"If my father were here today, I can only imagine how disappointed he would be to hear this, how disappointed he would be in *you*," Robecca stated honestly.

"Trust me, your father made his disappointment more than clear to me," Ramses answered.

"He knew? Is that why he's no longer here? Where is he? What did you do with him?" Robecca screamed.

"This is absolutely shocking!" Miss Flapper cried out dramatically as she threw her hands in the air.

"Oh, can it, Sylphia! We wouldn't even be in this situation if you had pulled off the Whisper like you were supposed to," Tab Bee hissed as only a werecat can.

"Well, at least I didn't kidnap my own child," Miss Flapper shot back.

"No, you just kidnapped our former intern after failing to properly control her," Ramses de Nile growled.

"Oh, please! Wydowna's having a grand time in the old maze with Bloodgood and your divas! It's not like she's suffering!"

"First, I want to thank you guys for basically interrogating each other. It makes my job a whole lot easier. But now I am going to have to take you three downtown with me," Scariff Fred interjected as he motioned for one of his deputies to handcuff Miss Flapper, Ramses, and Tab Bee.

"Royalty in jail! Never!" Ramses screamed as he stormed out of the Study Howl with Miss Flapper and Tab Bee hot on his tail.

"Well, now we know why he wasn't on that list in the attic. He no longer considered himself a member of the Society of United Monsters. He had reverted to ASOME," Venus said as she shook her head at the scene that had just unfolded.

"What do you think he did with my father?" Robecca asked softly.

"Maybe he's in the old maze with the others," Cy suggested.

"Where is the old maze?" Robecca asked. "I've never even heard of it."

"Beneath the new one," Miss Sue Nami grunted, before lowering her head in shame. "I owe you non-adult entities an apology. You were right . . . again."

"No need for apologies. Just help us find Headmistress Bloodgood and the others," Rochelle replied.

"Speaking of apologies," Skelita interrupted, tears streaming down her black-and-white face. "*Lo siento*. I am so sorry. We didn't know. We thought Senorita Flapper was our friend, our mentor. I considered her an older sister. . . ."

"I am deeply ashamed by our behavior. We blindly followed that woman, never once stopping to question her actions or motivations. But, ghouls, you must believe us. We had no idea what she was up to," Jinafire offered solemnly, her head lowered to conceal her tears.

"We know, *chéries*," Rochelle replied kindly. "Madame Flapper is a very charismatic woman with a very charismatic wardrobe—falling under her spell is easy, especially when you are new to a place and looking for guidance."

"How can you be so understanding? We supported a woman who tried to ruin Monster High," Skelita babbled while dabbing her eyes.

"Yeah, but you ghouls didn't know that," Venus added. "Plus, you're hardly alone in having trusted Miss Flapper. She almost destroyed Monster High with the Whisper, and yet she was still able to convince the entire school that she was trustworthy!"

"In other words, don't lose any steam over it! We know you're good ghouls with good hearts, and frankly that's all that matters," Robecca explained, before offering the two distraught ghouls a genuine smile.

"Non-adult entities, I hate to break up this scarepy session, but need I remind you that Headmistress Bloodgood and the other ghouls still need rescuing?" Miss Sue Nami barked as she broke into a head-to-toe shake, sending drops of water every which way.

"Might we be of assistance in rescuing the others?" Jinafire asked, lifting her head for the first time.

"Thanks, but I think we got this," Robecca answered as she turned and looked at her friends—Rochelle, Venus, and Cy.

CHAPTER fourteen

finding a way down to the old maze was no easy task, as it had been long sealed off. In fact, after hours and hours of struggling and failing to locate the manner in which Miss Flapper, Tab Bee, and Ramses had entered, it was decided that they would simply have to burrow into the old maze using a mechanical drill from Grind 'n' Gears.

"Drills and chills! Am I the only one worried

225

that we might accidentally tunnel straight into Headmistress Bloodgood, Wydowna, Cleo, or Toralei?" Robecca asked with steam pouring out of her ears.

"Non-adult entity, for the last time, do not talk while I drill," Miss Sue Nami said as she manned the large metal contraption in the middle of one of the maze's many paths.

"Madame Sue Nami has assured me that this operation is safe. For as you know, safety is always my first priority," Rochelle calmed Robecca. "Now, might it be that you're feeling extra anxious right now because you're worried about your father?"

"My father?" Robecca repeated.

"Yes, I imagine you are frightened that he might not be in there," Rochelle responded.

"It's just that with Ramses de Nile, Tab Bee, and

Miss Flapper having disappeared back to the Old World, if he isn't in here, we'll have no leads. I may never find out where he is," Robecca fretted.

"Scariff Fred said he has two of his best deputies on Miss Flapper, Ramses de Nile, and Tab Bee's trails. I'm sure they'll eventually catch them," Venus reassured Robecca as Miss Sue Nami paused for one of her infamous water-spraying shakes.

"How's it looking, Miss Sue Nami?" Cy asked as he wiped droplets of water off his cheeks.

"Just about through," Miss Sue Nami responded, and then resumed drilling.

And indeed she was. Within minutes, Cy, Robecca, Rochelle, Venus, and Miss Sue Nami were lowering themselves through a root-filled hole into what looked like an abyss of vines, both dead and alive.

"This is what happens when monsters ignore their gardening duties, when they turn their backs on their plants," Venus said as she shook her head.

"I am highly concerned about what might be living within these vines," Rochelle said as she used her flashlight to investigate. "Rats? Snakes? An underground hybrid?"

"Snats?" Robecca chimed in.

"*Pardonnez-moi?*"

"That's what we could call the hybrid. Snats! Or rakes!" Robecca offered enthusiastically.

"Non-adult entities, I hate to rain on this parade of faulty science, but there is absolutely no way that snakes and rats could crossbreed, as snakes eat rats for breakfast, lunch, and dinner. Now that is not to say that there couldn't be snakes and rats residing separately, that is absolutely possible."

"Great," Venus moaned sarcastically as Miss Sue Nami started to pull back the vines so that the group could move forward.

Miss Sue Nami, followed by Venus, Rochelle, Robecca, and Cy, started through the labyrinth-like setting, all the while each of them hoping the same thing: that Miss Flapper had been telling the truth when she mentioned the old maze, that it wasn't a ploy to throw them off the right path.

"Deary me, I have a bad feeling about this. I don't think anyone's down here. Not even any snakes, rats, or hybrids!" Robecca yelped to Cy.

"But if they're not down here, where are they?" Cy asked.

"That's the problem. We have no idea," Venus grumbled.

"Stop whining, non-adult entities. You haven't come this far, battled this much, to give up before the mission is complete. Now, we can turn around like quitters or we can search every corner of the old maze until we are certain that ma'am and the others aren't down here," Miss Sue Nami barked.

"Madame is most correct. We have fought very hard to get to this point and now we must persevere until we find them, until we bring them home," Rochelle responded.

Covered in a wide variety of splinters and scratches, the group trudged forward, pushing through dried-up hedges and tangle upon tangle of overgrown vines.

"There's something up ahead," Miss Sue Nami called out to the others. "A clearing."

There, among the dried brown hedges and wildly growing vines, was a circular dirt patch, which bordered on an old metal door covered in soil, dried leaves, and spider webs.

"It looks like no one's opened this door in years," Venus mumbled at the sight of it.

"Sadly, I agree," Rochelle seconded.

"Rusty gears! What a disappointment!" Robecca squealed, and then kicked at the door, her copper boot banging loudly against the metal.

"*Chérie*," Rochelle started to reply, when a knocking sound emanated from the door.

"Did I just imagine that?" Robecca yelped as she looked to the others.

"No!" Venus screeched happily as she ran toward the door. "Robecca? What do you say you give this thing a quick steam cleaning?"

"It would be my pleasure," Robecca replied as her nostrils flared and steam began pouring out.

Once the lock was clean, Venus assessed it, even trying to use her vines to open it.

"Allow me," Rochelle said as she wiped her claws against her shirt.

But after fiddling with the lock for a few minutes, the granite ghoul sighed loudly.

"*Zut!* I am not making any headway!"

"Move out of the way, non-adult entities," Miss Sue Nami announced as she ran full speed toward the door.

But even after the wall of water smashed against the metal door, the lock remained in place.

"I think I have an idea. It's far-fetched, but you never know," Cy offered.

"Run at it again?" Miss Sue Nami suggested.

"No," Cy said as he turned and looked at Robecca. "What did you do with that key we found in the catacombs? The one you said might unlock the mystery to finding your father."

Robecca slowly pulled out a chain from under her shirt, on which hung the rusted key.

"I held on to it like you told me, so I always remember to keep the faith," Robecca explained.

"The odds are not in our favor," Rochelle added. "But I certainly am hoping that we defy the statistics."

Robecca slowly walked up to the door and removed her necklace.

"Please be in here, Father," Robecca whispered as she inserted the key into the lock.

Never had the faint sound of a lock clicking

seemed so loud and thunderous.

"I'm speechless," Rochelle mumbled as the heavy metal door creaked open.

"Absolutely shocked, but in the best possible way," Venus added, and then winked at Robecca, who was first to enter the space.

Behind the door was a small but charming room decorated as if it were the inside of a genie's bottle, with purple satin walls, large gold pillows, and strands of beads dangling from the ceiling.

"Thank heavens you found us!" Cleo moaned as she walked toward Robecca, Cy, Rochelle, Miss Sue Nami, and Venus clad in an elegant hand-woven gown. "Not that it's been all bad. Check out what Wydowna made me. I mean, I have to tell you, she's more talented than Moanatella Ghostier and Calvin Cry'in combined."

"It's true. And now we feel super bad that we were so mean to the spider ghoul. She's actually pretty cool. Obviously not as cool as me, but then again that's impossible," Toralei admitted as she flounced across the room in a spooktacular lace dress.

"Um, actually it isn't, because I'm way cooler than you are. I'm royalty, in case you forgot."

"So? I'm a celebutante."

"Ghouls, sorry to interrupt, but is there anybody else here?" Robecca asked nervously, wringing her copper hands together.

"Of course, Headmistress Bloodgood and Wydowna are trying to break down the other door, the one that exits into the catacombs," Cleo answered.

"Wydy? Heady? Come in here, we've been rescued! And you'll never believe by whom! Those ghouls who used to drive me crazy, the wet lady, and the boy with the big eye," Toralei cried into the other room.

"Wow, those are some pretty colorful descriptions of us," Venus said with a laugh.

"Wydy? Heady?" Rochelle repeated back.

"Like I said, we've really bonded," Toralei explained.

"While I am very pleased to hear that, I would very much like to encourage you to find new nicknames for them both. I am sorry to say that Heady and Wydy are not very becoming," Rochelle advised Toralei.

Wydowna and Headmistress Bloodgood, who was also clad in a webbed creation, walked into the room and immediately broke into the biggest smiles possible.

"My ghouls! I knew you would find us!" Headmistress Bloodgood exclaimed.

"What about me, ma'am? Didn't you think I would find you?" Miss Sue Nami inquired.

"Not really, but only because I knew you would be terribly busy running the school," Headmistress Bloodgood responded diplomatically.

"Wydowna, how are you holding up?" Cy asked, and then motioned toward Cleo and Toralei, who were both checking their makeup in a nearby mirror.

"You know, it's a funny thing, but once you get to know them you realize that they don't mean half the things they say. And, well, that makes it a whole lot easier to be ghoulfriends," Wydowna explained candidly.

"Robecca, dear, you needn't worry anymore,"

237

Headmistress Bloodgood said as she looked at the downcast ghoul. "We are all safe and sound."

"Yes, but is anybody else in here?" Robecca asked as steam started to pour out of her eyes.

"What do you mean? Like our pets?" Cleo chimed in.

Rochelle and Venus instantly engulfed Robecca in their arms, holding tight, trying with all their might to absorb her disappointment.

"We won't give up!" Venus whispered in her friend's ear. "Not until we find him."

"Really?" Robecca blubbered.

"Really. We're ghoulfriends forever, remember?" Rochelle added.

"Yes, ghoulfriends forever," Robecca repeated back with a smile.

epilogue

wash in frustration and confusion over her father's betrayal to not only her but Monster High, Cleo decided that there was only one thing to do—turn his tomb into an extra closet. And though Ramses had written Cleo a letter apologizing for being led astray and promising to return to face his former friends and partners at the Society of United Monsters, Cleo continued with her renovations.

In the midst of packing her father's seemingly endless supply of finely tailored gauze suits, Cleo came across a mechanical box with hexagonal panels. Intrigued, she immediately started tapping and prodding the strange contraption. Almost instantly a panel popped open revealing a picture of a normie, attached to which was a thin blue envelope. Tucked neatly inside the blue paper was a map, only instead of leading to a pot of gold or a specific location, it led to a man: Hexiciah Steam.

Sensing an opportunity to not only right her father's wrongs, but possibly facilitate a family reunion for a ghoulfriend, Cleo quickly delivered the box to Robecca, Rochelle, and Venus.

ABOUT THE AUTHOR

As a child Gitty Daneshvari talked and talked and talked. Whether yammering at her sister through a closed door or bombarding her parents with questions while they attempted to sleep, she absolutely refused to stop chattering until finally there was no one left to listen. In need of an outlet for her thoughts, Gitty began writing, and she hasn't stopped since. Gitty is also the author of the middle-grade series *School of Fear*.

She currently lives in New York City with her highly literate English bulldog, Harriet. And yes, she still talks too much.

Visit her at gittydaneshvari.com.

Don't miss these defrightful activity journals for ghouls!

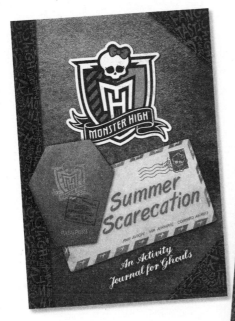

Don't miss the rest of the series!

And keep a lurk out for the
ghoulfriends' next fun book,

Coming fall 2014!